WATCHING THE WATCHER

Gaye Hiçyılmaz lived in Turkey for many years, much of that time in the city of Ankara, which provided the setting for her first children's book, *Against the Storm*. Inspired by a true incident in the Turkish press, it was first published in England, where it was shortlisted for the Whitbread Award in the children's fiction category and was runner-up in the Guardian Children's Fiction Award the same year. After leaving Turkey the author moved to Switzerland with her four children and for seven years lived in the small town of Horgen, which gave her the background for her second award-winning novel, *The Frozen Waterfall*. She now lives near Brighton in England.

Watching the Watcher

GAYE HİÇYILMAZ

ff

faber and faber

First published in 1996
by Faber and Faber Limited
3 Queen Square London WC1N 3AU
This paperback edition first published in 1997

Photoset by Avon Dataset, Warwickshire
Printed and bound in Great Britain by
Mackays of Chatham PLC, Chatham, Kent

© Gaye Hiçyılmas, 1996

Gaye Hiçyilmaz is hereby identified as author of this
work in accordance with Section 77 of the Copyright,
Designs and Patents Act 1988

*This book is sold subject to the condition that it shall not, by way of trade or
otherwise, be lent, resold, hired out or otherwise circulated without the
publisher's prior consent in any form of binding or cover other than that in
which it is published and without a similar condition including this condition
being imposed on the subesequent purchaser*

A CIP record for this book
is available from the British Library

ISBN 0-571-17274-1

For my parents,
Dorothy and Harry Campling,
who took us into the countryside

Chapter 1

'But they *were* ladies,' insisted Henry, 'carved ladies.'

'They couldn't have been.' His father, Mr Constable, was clear about that.

'Why not?' Henry, who had seen them, didn't understand.

'Well, Uncle Arthur isn't interested,' explained Mr Constable, scraping up the marmalade he had dropped.

'Not interested? Wow!' mocked Ed who was eleven and knew everything. 'Poor old Uncle Arthur! Not interested, eh?'

He pulled that sort of a face at his twin sister Emma and she choked on her muesli. Ed grinned. Em staggered to her feet with milk running out of her nose.

Mrs Constable put down the letter she had been reading and told them all to stop being so silly and Em to take a few deep breaths. Mr Constable glanced at his watch and took more toast and the rest of them exchanged looks.

Em made another revolting noise, like a boot stuck in mud, and her brothers and sisters shrieked 'Oh yuk!' and 'How disgusting!' and pushed back their plates. Anyway, it was time for the morning bathroom rush.

Only Henry sat on with his parents and re-read the letter that had unexpectedly arrived for him from his Great-Uncle Arthur.

'They *were* ladies,' he said doggedly. 'They were carved in something and very dark. I only saw them once but I did see them.'

1

'I'm sure you saw them, but I expect they were something else,' said his father. 'Your Great-Uncle Arthur is a scientist. Like I said, he's not interested in art. So eat up, time's getting on.'

Outside the kitchen window there was bright summer sun and other families were double locking their front doors and backing their cars out into the morning rush-hour. It was almost the end of term.

The twins came back into the kitchen and were crashing around getting their school stuff together. Mrs Constable usually helped but today she sat on at the breakfast table, poured herself more tea, and re-read her own letter.

'I didn't just see them,' continued Henry. 'I *felt* them and – '

This set Ed and Em off again and they fell about screaming 'He *felt* them' and rolling their eyes. Even Rose and Tom, who were older and past that sort of rubbish, smiled. Mrs Constable gave Mr Constable one of her looks but he only glanced at his watch again and got up. He always left her to deal with 'silliness'.

'I did,' said Henry loudly to his father's back. 'I really did see them. It was on that visit and I went up those wooden stairs to that very top bit where the sun was coming in.'

He could remember it clearly. The whole family had driven down to Roxmere Park to visit their father's uncle, Arthur Constable. Henry remembered climbing to the top of the house, where the stairs hadn't been carpeted or even painted at the edges. He had fiddled with both the attic doors but they had been locked, so he'd looked through one of the keyholes. Then he'd seen the statues. They were standing close together in the dim attic: a forest of heads and long curved backs and women's bodies. He'd looked away and sat down on the warm, dusty boards which were

2

knotted with knobbly whorls of cut-off branches. The sun had been slanting down in sharp squares from a high, barred window. It was very quiet up there. He'd traced an intricate pattern in the dust between the nail heads and one had been sticking out and had scratched his leg.

That dust had been so thick that he'd wondered if it wasn't actually something else, like animal fur, and he'd bent right down to have a closer look and then had seen the crack under the attic door. It was a gap more than a crack. He'd lain down flat, getting dust up his nose, and he'd poked his hand and then his arm under the door. It had gone in up to the shoulder.

He had touched the carvings, shutting his eyes and letting his fingers slip and slide.

Then he had felt hair: touched it with the tips of his fingers and, horrified, jerked his hand quickly back and –

'Henry!' cried his mother, leaping to her feet.

'Mother, I'm sorry.' He had swung his arm and knocked the cup from her hand.

She didn't look at him but began to dab at her skirt. The twins protested noisily and flicked drops of tea from their rucksacks.

'I'm really sorry.'

'For heaven's sake, Henry, just be quiet!' exploded Mrs Constable.

'But I didn't – '

'Oh yes you did. As always. You always have to keep on and on about things, don't you?' There were marks on her blouse too. 'I don't care if Uncle Arthur has rooms full of carved . . . carved . . .' She was floundering. She needed an animal that wouldn't set the twins off again.

'Guinea-pigs?' suggested Rose helpfully.

'Exactly.'

3

Henry stared at them all in amazement. 'Guinea-pigs?'

'Henry, I'm warning you!' She was working furiously at the stains. 'Now I'll have to go upstairs and change!' And she did, but turned back and added: 'Just you go upstairs too and clean your teeth. If anyone in this family needs to, it's you.'

'Oh come on, Mother,' his elder brother Tom was roused to protest, but Mrs Constable wasn't having it. Henry trailed upstairs to the bathroom.

It really wasn't fair. He inspected his teeth in the mirror. He knew he'd only got two fillings. His teeth might be a bit crooked, but they weren't rotten. They were like his father's teeth which were also rather crowded at the front. He looked at himself critically: brown-haired, taller than average, but a bit slouchy. A bit pink and white too, if he were honest. He was definitely not one of the lads. He wished he looked more like Tom who was fair and pale and hungry looking, even though he had a few spots.

Henry knew that he looked like his father. The trouble was, he didn't feel like him. Not at all.

He was still staring at himself when Tom hurried into the bathroom and edged him aside. Tom was really into things like mouthwash and dental floss and deodorants. Their mother always complained that he used hers.

'They *were* women,' repeated Henry, to the mirror.

'What were?' Tom mumbled through a mouthful of foam.

'The carvings were. They *were* carvings of women. You know, real women.'

'Aah.' Tom, who was eighteen and should know, rinsed his mouth.

'Look here, Henry, don't take any notice of Mother. She was just in one of her moods this morning.'

4

'Why? I haven't done anything.'

'Of course you haven't.' Tom spat cheerfully. 'I think that letter upset her.'

'What? My letter from Uncle Arthur?'

'No, no. Well, yes, maybe that as well, but I'm sure it was that other letter from Epsteins which really upset her.'

'From Epsteins?' It was the department store in town. They always bought their school uniform there.

'Yes. She applied for a job there ages ago, at Easter or so, and I'm only guessing, but I think that letter this morning was a rejection.' Tom laughed. 'Probably told her she was too old or something. That's what's put her in a bad mood again.'

Henry looked at his teeth. It felt disloyal, listening to talk like that about his mother, even if it was true.

'Well, I'm off,' said Tom, patting his hair into shape, and Henry heard him run down the stairs, whistling.

He hadn't known that his mother had applied for a job. It was an odd thing to have done because she always said that there was too much to do at home. And she did do a lot. She was the sort of mother who baked her own bread and made lemonade out of real lemons. She took a close interest in everything they did and was always helping with projects and homework. People at school, whose mothers were never at home, thought he was really lucky.

Still, he was glad it wasn't his letter she was angry about. He didn't particularly want to go and stay with his Great-Uncle Arthur in Roxmere Park, but it had been nice to be asked. He hardly ever got letters, let alone an invitation like this.

He ran the tap noisily. That'd make her think that he was cleaning his teeth. He even wet his toothbrush and smeared toothpaste on the basin, in case she challenged him, but he needn't have bothered.

She wasn't in the kitchen when he went down. Everyone seemed to have gone. Someone had stacked the dishwasher. The house was empty.

'Mother?' He couldn't believe it. She always said good-bye.

'Mother?' He unlocked the back door and looked out and called, but she didn't answer. Poor old thing! Tom must be right. That letter from Epsteins must have really upset her. She would be sulking somewhere: when she was really annoyed with them she often went down to do things to the compost heap. It was probably better not to disturb her.

He wandered back into the kitchen, and ate a piece of cold toast. She could hardly have gone off somewhere, because it was too early. Even Epsteins didn't open till 9 a.m.

It took Henry a moment or two to realize that the kitchen clock said 9.30 a.m. He thought he must have misread it; then, that it had gone wrong. It could have stopped yesterday. It could have been Ed, playing a joke and turning the hands on, to scare them. It could have been anything if his own watch hadn't said 9.35 a.m.

The first lesson ended at 10.10 a.m! He tore out of the house, then remembered that the first lesson on Tuesday was French. Now that the teacher had to speak in French, being told off wasn't so bad. When she shouted at him he wouldn't understand, and if she asked him why he was late he wouldn't be able to explain.

Nevertheless, he wouldn't have minded seeing a bus in the distance, because after French it was PE. He was on the bus, upstairs, when he realized that he'd dashed out without his PE kit. 'Not just late, but stupid as well.' That was what Mr Rory would say.

He did too. He stood with legs apart and hands on hips, and bawled from across the hot field.

6

Henry, who was now fractionally taller than Pig Rory, walked slowly towards him over the running lanes. The PE teacher was a stocky, noisy man who liked to go around the school dressed in shorts, whatever the weather. He was proud of his thighs: great white mountains of muscle covered with little yellow hairs. They quite overhung his knees, which were pink and wrinkly, and it was these knees that Henry needed to keep his eyes on. He had discovered on other, disastrous occasions that there was something about the smallness of Pig Rory's head, perched like an afterthought on his thick, musclebound neck, that made him want to giggle.

Today, listening to the usual stuff about being lazy and having the wrong attitude, Henry felt hard done by. He wouldn't have forgotten his kit if his mother hadn't disappeared like that. She always remembered for him, for all of them, actually. She would stand by the door chanting: 'Isn't it clarinet today, Rose? . . . Tom, don't forget your racquet . . . Emma! Thursday! . . . Ed, remember that Peter's mother is bringing you home after drama club.' She even remembered things for their father, who joked that she should have been in the secret police because she always knew where everything in the house was, or should be.

To be quite truthful, she had to remember much more for the others than she did for him, because the others had interests. Henry didn't. All the Constable children were busy and talented and got interested in things, except him. He just got bored.

Henry suffered from boredom like other people suffer from colds. Boredom crept up on him like a sore throat in the evening. He would start off on something new, something that they all thought was really 'him'. Then he'd feel bored. It had always been like that, with stamps and modelling and even with butterflies.

He'd just discovered how to kill them – with mothballs in a screw-top jar – and he'd mounted a few on a bit of wood, when his mother had brought home some lovely library books on butterflies and moths. The illustrations were superb but, as she bent over his shoulder, helping him identify what he'd found, he had begun to feel desperately bored. He just wasn't interested. He even avoided the garden because his family began calling him over to 'come and look'. There was always something he 'had to see', and it wore him out.

They'd given him a beautiful specimen case for his twelfth birthday, even though he'd tried to tell them that he wasn't interested in butterflies any more. Now the case stood in his bedroom, dusty, expensive and reproachful.

This year, for his thirteenth, they'd given him a watch, a 'grown-up' watch. It told the time in different parts of the world and withstood water pressure to 100 metres.

'It'll be so useful,' said his father, 'for diving – or anything.'

Mr Constable was right, of course, except that Henry couldn't dive.

He was thinking about this while Pig Rory bellowed at him.

'And I can tell you, Henry Constable, it might be the last week of term, but I'm not going to forget this. And if I have the bad luck to get landed with you next year, when you're a Year 9, then, my lad, you'll have to change your attitude!'

Henry looked up. He heard the murmur of disapproval from the class, who were fed up standing around listening. Everybody knew that old Henry was hopeless at games. Why couldn't Pig Rory leave him alone and let them get on?

Henry rashly looked into those small, pale-lashed

eyes and that upturned snout of a nose – and lost it. He smiled.

'And you can wipe that idiot's grin off your face, because next term –'

'I shan't be here next term,' said Henry suddenly, surprising even himself.

'Oh no?' snorted the Pig, and stepped back.

'Yes. I mean no,' he stammered. The class moved closer. 'I'm going away,' said Henry. He knew he'd gone bright red, but it was too late. 'I'm going away to stay with my uncle. He's invited me.'

'More fool he,' said Mr Rory nastily, and walked off.

By lunch time Henry Constable was a minor celebrity, and Julie Richards and her friend Tanya actually sat either side of him at the table.

Even Mrs Silk, their form teacher, had heard something. She paused at Henry's name as she struggled through the afternoon register.

'A little bird told me that we may be losing you, Henry,' she said coyly, to a chorus of cheers, and she continued to smile encouragingly at him even when somebody said 'little pig more like' and snorted.

Henry's jaw dropped in horror. He couldn't speak.

'It's putative,' said Adam Draper politely, leaning back in his chair and smoothing his nicely combed hair.

Mrs Silk scowled over her frown. She had never trusted Adam, who was too clever for his own good and didn't have to struggle enough.

'You know I don't allow language like that in my classroom, Adam Draper, and anyway I'm sure Henry can speak for himself. Can't you, dear?' Mrs Silk was good (she always said) with shy boys. 'It's a big step, changing schools at this stage. Quite a challenge.'

He nodded and blinked at her through a huge, suffocating yawn that made his eyes water.

'Years ago I heard your uncle give a lecture at the zoo – in Regent's Park!' Her voice rose shrilly to cut through the outburst of animal sounds. 'He was a wonderful speaker, Henry, so dynamic: one of the first conservationists. I remember him arguing so passionately for a sense of order and the need to keep things as they are. It'll be a great opportunity for you, Henry . . .'

But he wasn't listening. He was fighting his way out through the incoming class, and Mrs Silk was left with her register unchecked.

Chapter 2

Henry often walked home with his neighbour, Adam Draper. Adam was easily the brightest person in their class, not counting Amy Manning, and Amy Manning didn't count because she was a swot. The girls said that she never lifted her nose from her books. Adam, in contrast, was a hero: a rebel who had had his ear pierced in Year 7 and who still got top marks. And his mother was odd.

They walked back together, spending the bus fare on food and still getting home almost on time because the roads were so clogged up with traffic.

'The thing is,' muttered Henry, 'I just said it to annoy the Pig. I don't really want to go and stay with my uncle. Anyway, my parents wouldn't let me. And I'm not going to stay away, whatever Silky thinks.'

Adam nodded and held out the bag of chips. That was the thing about Adam. He understood what people were saying without them having to say it all.

'You know, you don't have to go, or tell anyone anything,' said Adam at last.

'But they'll ask . . .'

'So? Let them. It's nothing to do with anyone else. And if Pig Rory or Silky asks you why you didn't go, you can lie.' He shrugged. 'Tell them that your uncle got ill.'

It was the perfect solution.

'He's pretty old, isn't he?'

'I suppose so. He's my father's uncle, so he's my great-uncle. He must be seventy now.'

Adam chucked the empty bag into a bin.

'There you are. That's if you really don't want to go.'

'I don't. Not really.'

'Might be fun.'

'Fun?'

'Why not? You'd get away from here . . . from this.'

It was a particularly hot, dusty afternoon, and so noisy in the street that they had to raise their voices. The air smelt of dirty pavements and old buses.

'I'd go,' said Adam unexpectedly, 'if it wasn't for Mum.'

Henry nodded and they walked on in silence. His own mother would be waiting at home now, with tea laid on the kitchen table. It wasn't like that at the Drapers.

And it wasn't like that at his home either. Mrs Constable was there in the kitchen, but so was a policeman. He was standing in the middle of the kitchen, drinking a cup of tea. Mrs Constable was taking scones out of the oven. Henry, who had felt odd when he first saw the police car outside their home, now felt better. It couldn't be death or anything, not with scones and tea.

'You're back, Mother,' he said.

'Obviously,' she replied, her voice icy in that warm, tea-time kitchen.

'And this is?' The policeman looked at Henry and then at his notes.

'Henry,' replied his mother.

They were both staring at him and Henry glanced around the kitchen, to avoid them. It looked tidier than usual. His mother had probably cleared up or rearranged things; she was always busy at home, which was why Rose called her 'Supermum'.

'Henry,' said Mrs Constable, 'the police want to know what time you left for school this morning.'

'It was . . .' he paused, wishing that Rose or one of the others would come home.

'Was it later than usual?' asked the policeman.

'Yes.' He didn't look at his mother. 'It was after 9.30 a.m.'

He heard her sigh.

'I see. And I understand from your Mum here, that this morning's routine was a bit different.'

Henry nodded. He felt quite odd again. Surely Emma should have been home by now? All that 'don't talk to strangers' stuff flashed uncomfortably through his mind, even if she was a pest.

'So what was different about this morning?'

'I got an invitation from my great-uncle.'

'Henry, do you have to be so stupid?' His mother was clearly upset.

'After that, Henry. After breakfast,' said the policeman patiently. 'Your mum says that she had to go out early, in a hurry. She left you in the house alone. Now that was unusual, wasn't it?'

'I expect she forgot,' said Henry cautiously. He looked from one to the other and felt dreadful. He suddenly guessed what was happening. 'She didn't mean to leave me alone.' There had been a case like this on the news: a woman had been sent to prison for leaving her child alone in the house. No wonder his mother was so jumpy. It was really unfair of the police because she wasn't a bad mother at all. She was too good, if anything. The bad mother on their street was Mrs Draper.

'I don't think she really went out,' protested Henry loyally. 'I just couldn't see her. She was probably here all the time, and I didn't look properly.' He glanced at her, giving her a

13

chance. 'You *were* down near the compost heap, weren't you?'

'Of course I wasn't down near the compost heap! I was on my way to Epsteins – '

'So you looked for her in the garden, eh?' The policeman smiled at Henry encouragingly.

'Yes.'

'Did you open the back door?'

'Yes, I unlocked it and looked out.'

Mrs Constable sighed, loudly.

'I'm home!'

They all heard Em storm in, sling her rucksack on to the hall seat, kick off her shoes and dive into the sitting room. Then they heard her shriek and come running out.

'Mum, where's the telly? It's *Neighbours*. Mum?'

Then she saw the policeman in the kitchen.

'Mum? Where's the microwave? And your radio – and Mum, where's my tape deck? I left it there, on the shelf, last night! Mum?' She dashed away upstairs to check her bedroom, and the policeman asked Henry, very kindly, if he could remember relocking the back door.

He couldn't.

'Of course he can't!' sighed Mrs Constable, bitterly.

'Now you mustn't blame him,' said the policeman. 'The burglars would have probably broken in anyway: kicked the door in or smashed that window, and then you'd have had all that damage, as well as the losses.'

It was decent of him to try, but Mrs Constable was not to be won over. She still stood there, holding the tray of scones and shaking her head in what Henry thought was dumb fury, but when he looked again he saw that she was actually crying. That made him feel even worse.

She didn't say much that evening but he knew what she was thinking: it was all his fault. The burglary was all his bloody, stupid, idiotic, selfish, lazy fault. It was what they must all think.

Certainly that was Mr Constable's opinion. He had come back already irritated by a sticky, much delayed rush-hour train and had barely put a foot into his front garden when the twins rushed out to tell him that they had been burgled and had 'lost everything, absolutely everything'. When, grim-faced, he discovered that the insurance policy didn't cover them because the house had been left unlocked, he was simply furious.

'See? See?' he shouted at Henry, thrusting the insurance documents under his nose. 'Do you think insurance companies are fools?'

'I don't know.' It was true, he didn't. All those things that his parents talked about, such as tax, insurance, train timetables and the health service, just seemed to be part of that inexplicable and unapproachable adult world that lay in wait somewhere in the boring grey distance.

'Honestly, Father, I was in a hurry, I didn't think about anything.'

'I know that, Henry. You don't have to tell me and your mother. We know you don't think about anything! In fact, we're beginning to wonder if you even know how to think!'

'Come off it, Dad,' said Tom.

Mr Constable looked at his eldest son over the top of his glasses.

'When I need your advice on how to bring up my family, I'll ask for it,' he said pompously.

Em and Ed made smug faces at each other.

Rose was nice about it too, even though she'd lost loads of things. All her rings and jewellery were gone, as was her camera and, it seemed, some expensive perfume. The burglars had tipped her clothes out on to the floor and made her pretty, flowery room into a real pigsty. Nevertheless she seemed to think it was just bad luck, and later that evening she admitted that she had left the back door unlocked lots of times. Tom had lost things too, but his room was so untidy that he wasn't sure what had actually gone.

Ed and Em appeared to have lost more things than they actually owned, and they complained endlessly. Ed had found traces of white powder on his carpet and he had scooped it into an envelope. He knew, without a shadow of doubt, that it was cocaine. If he hadn't lost his new trainers, he'd have enjoyed the excitement.

Only Henry did not seem to have lost anything. His room was almost as he had left it. The drawers were pulled out and his wardrobe disarranged, but he could find nothing missing at first. Only later that evening did he discover that his knife had gone, but he couldn't mention it. He had kept it hidden under the floorboards together with a magazine with pictures of nude women that he'd found thrown over a hedge last year. He didn't understand how a casual burglar had found it. What was even odder was that they'd only taken the knife. The magazine was still there – though moved, he was sure.

'But why didn't they take any of Henry's stuff?' asked Emma, yet again, at supper.

'He's so boring he hasn't got anything worth taking,' said Ed, sourly. His mother had only bought him the trainers last week.

'Oh shut up,' said Tom. 'He hasn't lost as much because he hasn't got as much. He's not as greedy as you two!'

'I'm not greedy. I just need a lot of things,' said Ed.

'Like £80 trainers?'

'They're not trainers, they're running shoes. Anyway, Mr

Rory says that athletes need decent equipment to improve their performance.'

'All right, Ben Jonson.'

'Mum! Tom called me Ben Jonson!'

'Now do be quiet, both of you,' said Mrs Constable. 'Don't make things worse by quarrelling. We've all been upset quite enough!'

'They cracked my specimen case,' muttered Henry, feeling he had to contribute some damage.

'Honestly, Henry!' Mrs Constable's voice trembled. 'They could have smashed that lovely thing to smithereens for all you seem to care!'

It was then that he almost told them about the knife, but stopped just in time. Adam had given it to him last Christmas holidays and Henry had always had a nasty feeling that it might have been pinched. It was a commando knife and would have cost pounds, or at least a lot more than Adam ever seemed to have. Mrs Constable always said that Mrs Draper never paid the milkman on time.

He should have told someone, because a knife like that could do damage, but he didn't. They just kept going on and on about the burglary and the insurance and how it wasn't 'just a matter of money'. All he wanted to do was escape. He couldn't be bothered to explain about the knife and he was bored out of his mind.

He went up to his room early and flopped out on his bed and understood what people meant when they said they were bored to death. He always felt boredom as some pressing, syrupy ache over his nose and forehead, but burying his face in his pillow rarely made it any better. It was a hot evening, much too hot to be going to bed early, but he shut his eyes and lay perfectly still. He could hear the sounds of other families out in their back gardens. Someone was playing table tennis and he was sure that the music and laughter were from the Drapers, three houses down.

Mrs Draper would probably still be in her bikini on a night like this. She'd have friends round, not local people, but strangers. Some were foreigners. People said that on sunny afternoons she'd come to the front door with just a man's shirt on. It wasn't as though she were young and pretty like some people's mothers. No, she was thin and scrawny, with teeth like a horse, and skin like brown cardboard, his father always said. Mrs Constable always corrected him and said that Alison Draper wasn't so bad for her age, especially for someone who'd had a rough start in life. She just had one of those voices which carried, which is what you expected in a singer.

Nobody in their street had ever heard her sing, but they'd heard her laughter, and Henry could hear it now, slipping through the gap under the curtains and entering his neat, dull room.

He didn't know if it was the laughter that woke him, but something did. He was suddenly awake with a dream – or nightmare – melting from him beyond recall yet he had heard the sound of a knife on stone, as though someone had slid the blade around outside his window.

'I'm sorry,' his mother repeated quietly but clearly, down on the patio, 'but he does.'

'He'll grow out of it,' said his father. Then he added, but not pleasantly, 'And if he doesn't there'll be trouble.'

'Well, he'd better hurry up,' snapped his mother, and then there was that noise, which he now recognized as the sound of her trowel striking stones as she weeded. 'Because,' she continued, 'he's driving me crazy. I know he shouldn't, but he does. Everything that boy does annoys me!'

He could hear her trowel dashing about the rockery, stabbing the weeds to death. He eased himself up from his bed, crept over to the window and crouched there, breathing in the scent of honeysuckle and listening to what his mother was saying about Ed. He knew she found his younger brother's sense of humour annoying: they all did. Rose had gracefully christened it 'Ed's lavatorial phase'. Actually, some of the things he said were really funny, even if none of them dared laugh.

'Do you know, James, I'm dreading these summer holidays.' His mother sighed.

'But you've got things planned. You told me all about them,' said his father.

'Not for him I haven't,' said Mrs Constable grimly. 'He won't do anything.'

Henry felt cold. Suddenly on that hot night, something in his stomach clenched like a fist and he shivered miserably.

'You know what he's like,' continued his mother. 'He'll just sit around all day with that awful Draper boy. All they ever do is watch television.'

'Not now they won't,' growled Mr Constable.

Henry would have slunk away if he could, but he was held there as firmly as a poor bedraggled moth on a pin.

'Look, you'll just have to ignore him,' said Mr Constable, who was good at ignoring things.

'Ignore him!' cried Mrs Constable, and he heard her toss the trowel away so that it jangled and jumped across the neat stone slabs. 'You might as well ask me to ignore a great big splinter under my nail!'

Henry shivered and finally crawled back to bed, pulling the duvet up as though it were the depths of winter.

He tried to sleep and couldn't, yet wouldn't answer when Tom knocked on the door which separated their two rooms.

Tom came in anyway and rummaged around, looking, he said, for stuff to put on a gnat bite. Henry said that he hadn't got any, and his voice was so much more squeaky than he'd intended that Tom pulled the duvet away to investigate.

'Hey, come on,' he said, putting on the light, 'it's not as bad as all that.'

'It is,' sniffed Henry.

'It's just – you know, Mum. And Dad. They're upset. I bet they've left doors unlocked before now. It'll be better tomorrow.' He meant well, but of course he didn't know about the splinter under the nail. 'It was just bad luck, like Rose said and the police. I bet the burglars went to the Drapers, took one look at the lovely Alison in her nightie and fled screaming.' Henry smiled, in spite of himself. It was a little bit true. He'd been nervous of Mrs Draper when she first moved in. She always smelt really strongly of perfume and he'd hated that, then. She'd shaken his hand when Adam introduced them and he'd felt the brittle, papery scratch of her long, thin, red nails. Now he was used to her. Last Christmas she'd given him one of his nicest presents. It was a perspex box filled with brilliantly coloured liquids. When you shook it the colours bubbled and oozed and flowed, yet never quite mixed. He had really liked it. You didn't have to do a thing with it, only watch as the purple fell and folded into the violent, spiralling green.

And that had been taken, too. He knew instantly, even before he rolled over and looked at the empty space on his shelf. And then, when Tom had gone back to his own room, Henry buried his face in the pillow and cried bitterly.

Chapter 3

'Why, Henry!' exclaimed Mrs Draper when she opened the door to him early next morning. 'How nice.'

He didn't know what to say and so followed her into the kitchen.

'Henry! What's up?' Adam, who was eating cold curry for breakfast, was equally surprised. If Henry called for Adam he rarely came into the house, but waited outside. He didn't mind waiting, he said.

Mrs Draper pointed to a stool beside the table but he stood stranded in the doorway and blurted it out like some dumb kid.

'We got burgled yesterday!'

It was the sort of thing that Ed would do, and he could have kicked himself, but fortunately Ali Draper didn't seem to think he was dumb. She got up very slowly, as though she were really tired, and put her arm around him and stroked his hand as though he were, too. Then she nudged the stool again with her thin, bare foot, drew her bathrobe together and leaned forward, ready to listen.

So he told them. He even mentioned her stolen present but immediately regretted it because at once she started talking about replacing it. He hadn't intended that. In fact he hadn't intended to talk about the burglary at all, and so to change the subject he handed her the letter from his Uncle Arthur.

Adam leaned across the table and mother and son read

it together, his neat, dark head touching her bleached, tangled curls.

'How nice,' she said, 'that he wants you to stay. How flattering, Henry.'

'Oh, it's not really, Mrs Draper. He invites one of us every summer. It used to be Tom and then Rose, but they never went. It isn't specially me he wants. It's just my turn.' He needed to be honest: there was something so fragile about her that you had to be extra careful.

'Why didn't the others go?' asked Adam, now eating bread and jam, straight after the curry.

'They've always got too much on and my mother and father weren't keen. They said it wasn't suitable.'

'Then you should go,' said Ali Draper, with a smile. 'At once.'

'But he's really old now and the house is miles from anywhere. I might be lonely.' Henry found himself repeating exactly what his parents had said.

'I'd still go,' said Ali Draper. 'I wish Adam's uncle would invite him to stay.'

'See!' Adam protested cheerfully. 'She can't wait to get rid of me!'

'That's right.' His mother smiled at him, and stretching out her hand, messed up his combed hair. He didn't move away.

'But I really would go,' she continued. 'After all, he's quite famous.'

'You've heard of him, then?' Henry had not expected that.

His family all knew that Arthur Constable had been a famous naturalist and explorer but Henry hadn't realized that anyone still remembered him. Nobody at school had ever heard of Roxmere Park and its collection of wild animals, apart from Mrs Silk.

22

'And I know his son, Julian,' Ali Draper murmured softly.

'Do you?' Henry hardly knew Julian himself. He'd stayed with them a couple of times, but Henry couldn't remember much about him.

'He's Julian Constable the artist, isn't he?' asked Adam. His mother nodded.

'I didn't know he was a famous artist,' said Henry. 'I just thought he painted pictures.'

Ali Draper smiled, and her thin, pretty face was suddenly scarred with wrinkles. She poured herself more coffee with a frail, brown hand that looked like a little paw, except for its red, red nails. She hadn't touched the toast that Adam had made for her.

'Well, he isn't famous yet, but some people have heard of him. I know him because he was a fan of mine. He used to go to all our concerts and come backstage to meet the group. He was just a kid then – about the age of you two – but I followed his career.' She smiled again. 'You can't afford to neglect your fans, especially when you only have a handful.'

Henry was surprised. Once, Adam had shown him an old newspaper cutting about Ali Draper being mobbed at a concert. There seemed to have been hundreds of fans that night.

'My mother doesn't think much of his pictures,' said Henry.

Ali Draper's smile broadened, but she didn't say anything.

'And Dad says he wouldn't have them in the house.'

'I can imagine. But what about you, Henry?'

'Me?' He didn't know what he thought.

She reached behind her and dragged something out from beside the fridge.

23

It was a woman's face: a dreadful tortured woman's face painted in thick slashes of colour, with the purple mouth open and screaming out of black skin. Ali Draper picked off the trailing bits of spider's webs and onion skins and stood the portrait up against the toaster.

'Well,' she said, 'what do you think, Henry?'

'I . . .' He was shocked.

'It seems a bit mean to stick it away down there, Mum,' said Adam. 'Why don't you give it to Henry? The artist is his relative, after all. It'll replace that thing he lost in the burglary.'

'Would you like to have it?' she asked gently.

'Yes. But I couldn't, Mrs Draper.' He was desperately embarrassed, but reached out to touch the thick, painted hair that was soft and gritty, as though the woman had lain in some gutter. 'They, they . . .'

'I see,' she said. 'Then I know what I'll do. I'll leave it to you. When you're older and have a place of your own, you can hang it there.' And she laughed.

'A place of my own?' He looked into her eyes. They were so dark that he couldn't see the pupils. 'All right,' he murmured.

He should have said thank you, but she might as well have been talking about hanging the picture on a nail stuck into the moon.

Adam was meticulously checking his schoolbooks. Ali Draper rested her chin on her hands and gazed at the picture.

'So you think I should go?' said Henry cautiously. She didn't seem to have heard but continued to stare at the portrait.

It made him feel uncomfortable. He knew that he would never have dared to take it home. His parents only liked pictures of things they knew: prints and watercolours of scenes and wildlife. In the living room there was a set of four prints of British owls. His mother had bought them at a car boot sale and framed them herself. She had hung them in a neat row above the sofa, because, she said, the browns matched. With horror Henry realized that yesterday evening these prints had not been there. He visualized the four jutting nails and the four pale patches on the wall beneath. This evening somebody else would notice.

'Wait a minute,' somebody would say, and they'd glance at the wall and then at him.

The policeman had warned them that it might be like this: over the next few weeks they would keep on noticing other things that had been stolen.

He knew then that he couldn't stand it. He had to escape.

When Adam went over to his mother and kissed her, Henry looked away, but she called after him.

'You should go, Henry. You really should.'

As they left, Ali Draper looked up at them from among the week's dirty dishes and scraps of food that still lay around the kitchen. The mess didn't seem to worry her. She just sat at the table, in the midst of it all.

They walked down the overgrown path and, as they hurried towards the bus stop, they heard her music leap out into the traffic in the busy summer street. Some brave voice rose up and soared over the dreary revving of hot engines.

'Next door will be complaining again,' laughed Adam. He didn't seem too bothered.

In fact Adam never seemed bothered by anything and Henry, who did, pushed his way awkwardly to the front of the overcrowded bus. Suddenly the attraction of that old and isolated house in that distant, walled park was intense.

Away from all this, with its bother and boredom, it must, he was sure, be better.

Stupidly, he didn't exactly know where Roxmere Park was, even though he'd been there. It was always like that. His parents would announce that the family was off somewhere and he, naturally, went along too, staring out of the car window at things he didn't want to see. He sometimes felt as though his eyes were overflowing with all those unsought scenes. It made him so tired that nowadays he fell asleep on car journeys and missed things, his parents said. They were always pointing out interesting sights that they had just passed by. They had probably pointed out all the important landmarks along the route to Roxmere Park but he'd missed them too.

He could only remember that the park had been near the sea and that its boundary walls had had something further built up on top of them. A safety fence, that was what his parents called it. It had been a high, mesh fence that was invisible at a distance, but which hummed and vibrated when the winds blew. He remembered the steep white cliffs as well. They had been forbidden to walk near the edge – not that he had wanted to, with the sea so far below. He could remember watching his mother walking ahead of him and holding the twins very tightly to either side of her, as though an unexpected gust might have grabbed them and dragged them over the edge. It was a treacherous place, his father had said, and not suitable for children, not suitable at all.

That was pretty well what they'd always said when the annual invitation came from Roxmere Park. Henry understood: of course they didn't want their precious children torn to bits by wild animals. They had repeated it all when his invitation had arrived but they hadn't really given it much attention. Everybody had automatically assumed that he wouldn't want to go. After all, Henry never wanted to go anywhere. Now, uncharacteristically, he had to persuade his parents to let him go.

'Not really,' said Adam, when Henry explained his difficulties to him after the first lesson that morning. 'You just have to get in first. Like in *Desert Storm*, you make a pre-emptive strike.'

'How do you mean?'

'You must accept the invitation straight away and make it impossible for your parents to back out afterwards.'

'How?' he asked tentatively.

'You phone him. Phone this old boy at once and tell him that you'd love to come and that your parents are absolutely thrilled. You know the sort of thing. Really lay it on. When do you want to go, anyway?'

'Today.' When he remembered the conversation about the splinter he still felt all shivery. If possible he would have left there and then, and not even gone into the next lesson. He'd walk away, with everyone staring and Mrs Silk calling helplessly: 'Henry Constable, come back here, and we'll talk about it!' He'd walk down to the station and get on the Roxmere train, ticket or no ticket, wherever Roxmere was.

'Go on then, phone.' Adam was already offering his phone card, but Henry had not got the letter with him and didn't know the number.

They made the call that afternoon from Adam's house. Alison Draper was not in but the letter was still there amongst the dishes on the kitchen table. When Henry picked it up it smelt faintly of curry. He dialled nervously. Listening to the ringing going on and on, Henry suddenly felt unbearably tired. He could have fallen asleep as he stood there. He yawned instead. Then, as he yawned again, a distant voice answered.

'Roxmere 6721? Hello? Hello?'

Henry, paralysed in mid-yawn, thrust the receiver at Adam.

'Hello?' The voice had sharpened.

'Hello? Uncle Arthur? It's me, Henry Constable!' Adam chattered away to Henry's uncle, relishing the part he was playing.

'Oh, *absolutely*, Uncle Arthur . . . yes . . . yes . . . no, I know they didn't . . . but I do, oh yes. No, no, they're *really* keen for me to come . . .'

He went on and on and then, with his hand over the receiver, he asked Henry if 'this Saturday would be all right?'

'This Saturday?' Henry was startled. It would be the first day of the holidays.

'Not after nine. No. No. No, I quite understand. Eight-thirty, then? Right . . . yes . . . yes . . .'

They both heard an abrupt click as the phone was put down.

'Wow!' Adam smoothed back his hair.

'Well?'

'Well – it's all fixed. You go down this Saturday and your parents have to phone him at eight-thirty this evening, to arrange the train times.'

'They'll kill me,' said Henry miserably.

'Rubbish. Anyway, they won't be the only ones with murderous intentions.'

'What do you mean?'

'I think that uncle of yours will happily tear you limb from limb if you phone him after nine o'clock.'

'Why?'

'He goes to bed! And nothing, absolutely nothing, is allowed to disturb him, he said. So, you've been warned!'

'Thanks, Adam. Thanks a lot.'

Chapter 4

If looks could have killed, Henry would have slumped forward and fallen across the table with his head in the pudding. The Constable family sat for several seconds in unaccustomed silence after Henry told them that he had accepted the invitation. Even Ed froze. As awkward moments go, this was bad. Henry had tried to tell his mother before, but she had been too busy preparing this special supper to 'cheer them all up' after the burglary. Normally he would have enjoyed chicken curry and strawberry shortcake but this evening it didn't taste good, and with the clock ticking on, he just came out with it.

Mr Constable raised one eyebrow and determinedly shaved off another sliver of shortcake.

'And you've got to phone him this evening, at eight-thirty,' Henry added. He knew that he should have said 'please', but his breath wouldn't go that far.

Half-way back to his plate Mr Constable's hand shook and the slice broke up and fell off the knife on to the clean white cloth.

Mrs Constable diverted her sharp gaze from Henry to the pink mess.

'Now look what's happened,' she said, and sighed bitterly. 'If people would only take proper slices . . .'

'I only wanted a taste,' Mr Constable began to scrape at the reddened wreck of cream and crumbs.

'That's what you always say! Now, for goodness' sake, James, let me cut you a decent piece.'

'I was leaving the rest for the children.' James Constable smiled innocently at his wife, 'You know how we all love your shortcake.'

'Nobody will love it now it's messed up!' she said in a hurt voice.

'Of course they will, dear!' He smiled brightly at the children. 'Emma? Tom? Ed?'

Henry wondered if he were invisible. Had they actually heard him speak at all?

Mr Constable was offering what was left but the children shook their heads. Mrs Constable gritted her teeth.

'Please, Mother. You must phone at eight-thirty,' Henry begged. Her indifference puzzled him. She was usually such an expert planner of expeditions. Their father always joked that she could have run Air Traffic Control without the computers.

'You must, Mother –'

'Oh I must, must I, Henry?' Mrs Constable grimly took on to her own plate the remains of the spoiled sweet that no one else wanted.

Then she looked up at him and, with her eyes fixed on his, slowly ate her first spoonful. Em sniggered.

'I didn't mean it like that, Mum. I meant . . .' Henry's voice trailed away. He watched her scraping up another mouthful and his courage failed. He hated scenes like this. Anything, death by firing squad, a slap on the face, would be better than this.

Her look was one of cruel reproach, and he felt the stab of it deeply.

'It doesn't matter, then. I won't go.' His voice was flat. 'I'll tell him.' He could have died, it was just such a bore.

Everything always was: things always dragged on into messes like this. Nothing was worth the bother.

His mother blotted her lips on her napkin and her face relaxed, but his father suddenly pushed back his chair.

'Oh no, Henry!' he said sharply. 'You can't wriggle out of it like that. You seem to think that you can do whatever you like and get away with it.'

'I don't.' It wasn't true. Henry never expected to get away with anything.

'It's no good protesting, because you know I'm right.'

'But, Father . . .' Tom made to leave the table, but his mother laid a finger on his hand and he sat down again impatiently.

'No, Tom, there are no "buts" about it. Henry has gone too far this time. Who does he think he is, arranging things behind our backs and ordering his mother about? And leaving that door unlocked, letting people in so that we've all lost things.'

'I haven't lost that much,' said Rose.

'Well I have!' shouted Ed. 'I've lost all my sports gear and my Walkman and my money-box and –'

'Shut up!' snorted Tom.

'Why should I?'

'Shut up!' Tom elbowed him.

'Mum! Tom hit me!'

In the middle of it all Henry looked at his watch.

'See? See?' cried his father. 'That's all you care about, your own convenience! You're totally selfish. You just want to swan off, without a thought for the rest of the family. Well, young man, you can go!'

'James!' Mrs Constable kept her napkin over her mouth.

'No, dear. I've made up my mind. If he wants to go, he can. We told him yesterday that we didn't think it was suitable, but he knew best. That's right, isn't it, Henry? You know best, don't you?'

'No.'

But this time he did and would have given all he had to have dared to say 'yes'.

'Now don't be modest: I'm sure you're much more experienced in managing your life than your mother and I, who have only brought up five children in the last eighteen years. So, young man – you know where the phone is. Or did the burglars remove that too?'

Ed and Em tittered.

Henry got up. He wished that the letter had never come, or had never been written, or that his parents had torn it up in disgust and cried 'no' straight away. It was what they had said to Tom and Rose in previous years. Then he remembered that other letter from Epsteins. It occurred to him that if his mother hadn't been so preoccupied with her letter, she would have paid more attention to his invitation and forbidden him to go.

'Well?' said Mr Constable.

'*You've* got to speak to him,' he muttered.

He looked imploringly at his mother, and as she took her napkin from her mouth he saw that she was half-smiling.

'Maybe a couple of days wouldn't be a bad idea,' she murmured quietly, and inspected her short, clean nails. She never painted them, unlike Ali Draper, because, she said, they chipped. 'You could stay half a week to please your uncle. Say Saturday to Friday, perhaps?' Her frown had quite gone.

At last he understood: she really did want him out from under her nice, neat nails.

'Certainly not more than a fortnight. And we will run you down,' she added. He wondered if she felt at all guilty.

'Of course we will,' agreed Mr Constable, looking relieved. 'I'll take you down myself.'

'You can't,' protested Ed. 'It's athletics. It's the County Meeting and you've got to take *me*.'

Then they went on and on about that and he just couldn't say that it was after half-past eight.

When the phone rang it startled them all, but Tom got there first. He was back so soon that Ed had only just begun giggling about some people's girlfriends being very keen. Henry was sure it had been a wrong number.

'Goodness,' said Tom, 'that was Uncle Arthur. He doesn't waste much time! Henry, you've to catch the 10.30 from Clapham Junction. Uncle Arthur says it's a direct line, so you won't have to change. Julian will meet you at Roxmere Station at 2.17.'

'I see,' said Mr Constable, coldly, 'You didn't think you ought to ask me or your mother first?'

'He didn't give me a chance,' retorted Tom. 'He put the phone down. But if you want to speak to him yourself, go ahead, Dad!'

They glared at each other, father and son, until Henry, desperate to escape, offered to do the washing-up.

The enormity of going to Roxmere Park did not really hit Henry until the Saturday morning of his departure. The end of term had all been such a rush. Normally he would have slept late on the first day of the holidays, but this Saturday he woke at dawn. The Constables had been going to the County Athletics Meeting for as long as he could remember, and it was always held on this Saturday. Mr Constable had been a middle-distance runner in his youth, not brilliant, he assured them, but useful. Ed, however, was going to be a star. He was a 'natural'. Everybody said so and today was his day. Today they would all watch Ed run and all clap when he got his medals.

All except Henry. He wouldn't be there. Even as they arrived at the station he couldn't quite believe it was happening. He'd never gone off on his own before. He had stayed in bed and listened to the street coming awake: to the chink of milk bottles put down and taken up and the swarming sound of cars moving out and crawling nose to tail all over everything. He would have liked to have gone then, to have just slipped away without fuss, and left the day to the rest of them and to Ed, but when he went downstairs his mother was already up and dressed, hard at work on his packed lunch. Now they insisted on staying with him until the train went, even though it would be cutting it fine for Ed's first race.

'I don't mind,' Henry said, and didn't. Actually he would have much preferred them to have gone. If they were so keen to get rid of him, why didn't they just drop him off in front of the station, like an unwanted dog kicked out of a car on to the motorway?

There had been one dreadful moment when they'd thought about asking the guard to 'look after him'. Luckily no guard appeared. Then Mrs Constable almost approached a young family in the same carriage, but to Henry's relief one of the toddlers kicked the mother on the shin and she swore and kicked him back. Mr and Mrs Constable moved away instantly.

All they had to do was go, but they wouldn't. They stood over him, getting in people's way and talking about embarrassing things like where the toilets were and putting one's ticket in a safe place, and not talking to anyone – well, anyone 'strange'. They kept on looking at their watches and then telling him that they had loads of time. Ed was pacing up and down the platform outside, knocking on the window, trying to force them to leave.

For once Henry wished Ed would get his own way.

He was saved by somebody decidedly 'strange'. A skinny old lady buttoned into a large blue coat scrambled up the steps into the carriage and made straight for the seat opposite Henry. She wore an odd blue hat that had slipped back off her head in the rush. There were plenty of other free seats, but she stood there determinedly, panting very slightly, even when his parents didn't step aside.

'I always go for young men,' she said, and leant towards Henry as though she were going to drop her suitcase in his lap. She smelt of something, or else her belongings did, and it took Henry a moment to realize that she wanted him to lift her case up on to the rack. It was very heavy.

'My son'll be glad,' she said to him as she waved vigorously to someone outside. 'He always tells me to find a strong young bloke who'll look after me on the train.' She smiled at him and he couldn't help smiling back.

The train jolted. Mrs Constable nodded meaningfully at some empty seats further up but he refused to understand. After reminding him yet again to phone as soon as he got to Roxmere Park, they hurriedly kissed him and patted his shoulder, and joined Ed on the platform. The train jolted again and he was off, watching them all grow smaller.

He shut his eyes and settled himself into the corner. He was afraid that the old lady would want to talk and he hated these sorts of conversations. She'd ask him how old he was and about his favourite subject in school. Then she'd ask about his family and what all his brothers and sisters did and she'd say that she had grandchildren just like him. But she didn't. He heard her scratching around in her carrier bags and muttering, and once her foot touched his, but he kept his eyes tightly closed.

He must have fallen deeply asleep because suddenly the sun was too hot on the side of his face and his heart thumped painfully.

He had missed Roxmere. He knew it— but it was only the refreshment trolley. The attendant was irritably reciting the prices of the drinks to the old lady.

'What's that? How much did you say coffee was?' She was looking into a battered old plastic purse.

'One twenty. And I don't make the prices, I just serve.'

'How much?' She was sorting through her change with awkward, trembling hands.

'One twenty! Now do you want anything or not?'

The man reminded Henry of some of the people who served school dinners.

'No. Not today, but thank you.' Her voice was thinner as she closed up the battered purse. Her lunch was already laid out on her lap: a couple of sandwiches – dried up at the edges, and with a smear of something in the middle – and a crushed pink wafer. Henry's mouth felt dry just looking at them. The carriage had become extremely hot.

The attendant glanced at him and Henry blushed. As he always did.

'May I have a Coke please, and –' He'd spoken too quietly and the man would have gone, but the old lady put out her hand to stop him. The cuffs of her coat were frayed so that a few white threads hung down her wrist. He took a breath and repeated loudly, too loudly, this time. 'A Coke, please. May I have a Coke and a cup of coffee?'

Please, please let her not protest.

And she didn't. Unbelievably, she just accepted it and didn't offer to pay or say a word about 'modern young people not being half as bad as people make out'. She just said 'thank you' really nicely as though he had done the most natural thing in the world, and he sipped the ice-cold Coke and felt very much better.

Beyond the window was a soft, summer bank with dog daisies amongst the grass and blue, blue sky above. There wasn't a road or wall in sight. Unexpectedly Henry found himself telling the old lady about his invitation to stay with his uncle. She nibbled at her sandwiches as she listened, saying at last, and very gently, 'But I thought Roxmere Park was all shut up now.'

'Oh no. My uncle still lives there. He still has some of his animals there.'

'I see,' she murmured. 'Of course my sister doesn't get up there any more. It's my sister I'm going to stay with. I try and visit her each summer for a couple of weeks.'

'That's what I'm doing. Staying a couple of weeks. At least,' said Henry cheerfully.

'Not going to miss your family then?'

'No! Not at all.'

'That's good,' she smiled. She wasn't that strange after all, only very, very poor.

'And that uncle of yours is coming to meet you, is he? At the station?'

'Oh yes. Well, not actually. His son Julian is. He'll meet me.'

'That's good.' She had packed away the rest of her meal and now her eyelids flickered down over her pale, tired eyes. 'I'm glad to hear someone is meeting you, because Roxmere Park is a lonely place and it would be a long walk up there. And people do say that there are other creatures there, in those woods.'

Then she folded her hands over her old, cracked handbag and the train moved slowly along the valley of the River Rox.

Chapter 5

Henry couldn't sleep. He looked out for landmarks, but recognized none. Anticipation made him restless. No one else had entered their carriage and his companion did not wake. Asleep, she looked even poorer, her shoes misshapen and odd and, as her grip on the handbag relaxed, he saw that its handle had been broken and was now bound up with string and Sellotape.

Beyond the glass the patterned greens and browns of farmland gave way to heath as the hills began to rise steeply on either side of the railway track. Now keen to see, he pressed his face against the window and felt the warmed glass cool as the valley sides steepened and cast shadows. Down below, now on one side, now on the other, he saw flashes of water from the River Rox. Once the train ran directly over it and he was startled by a drift of white clouds down there, between shaded, overhung banks.

He remembered the athletics meeting and wondered briefly if back up there the hot afternoon was also clouding over. He glanced at his watch. In less than five minutes they would be arriving. He hurriedly got his things together then swung down the old lady's case, but it was far too early and he was left swaying precariously in front of the train door with a case in each hand. He only just kept his balance as the brakes came on; the lady, woken by the jerk and screech, put out her frail arm to steady him.

'Have you seen the walls of the park?' she asked, and

when he shook his head she said that they were probably so overgrown by now that they had disappeared from view.

When the train drew into the station he peered up at the hillside, but still saw nothing of the boundary walls.

'If you're going to be in Roxmere for two weeks –' she began, but didn't finish in the jostle of getting down and looking around.

Her sister and brother-in-law were waiting on the platform and came hurrying up. Henry couldn't see Julian. He handed over her case and turned briskly away, not wanting to be thanked. He suddenly felt lonely but pretended to be busily occupied with the local timetables. He stood looking up at them and even traced an imaginary journey down the columns with one finger.

Julian still didn't appear. Henry began to feel through his pockets for the letter with the address and phone number, then stopped. Out of the corner of his eye he could see the old lady still standing on the platform, talking. She saw him too and waved. He frowned. He didn't want her to come over. He didn't want her to ask him if he had lost something or – even worse – ask if he was all right, because he wasn't. He felt really odd and panicky.

He should never have come. He'd been stupid to insist on coming without proper arrangements being made. His mother had warned him that it might all end in tears, but he hadn't listened. His parents usually made more fuss about sending the dog to kennels than they had done about this visit. They ought not to have let him come.

He turned abruptly away from the timetables and sat down on a bench. Julian would arrive soon, and was probably here already, if he got up and looked. But he couldn't. Instead he stretched out his legs, leant back and drummed his fingers along the top of the bench, very, very casually.

If he'd known the time of the next train back, he'd have crossed over to the opposite platform and caught it. He could be home in time for supper. And he wouldn't mind what they said. Not even Ed. Tomorrow he could begin again and it could be the first day of the holidays, almost.

He could just be at home, doing nothing. So long as he needn't be here and forgotten. Then he remembered that Julian had always been late for meals when he'd stayed with them. He had nearly driven his mother mad.

'Excuse me.' It was the old lady. Fortunately she did not seem to notice how miserable he was feeling. 'I forgot to give you my address.'

'It doesn't matter.' Henry knew he sounded rude.

'Of course it matters, dear. Do you think I'd let a gentleman treat me to coffee without giving him my address?'

He didn't know what to say or where to look. He supposed it was some sort of horrible, elderly joke. He didn't like her any more and would have got up and walked off if she hadn't sat down beside him and begun writing on the back of an envelope. She was even babbling on about him coming to tea. Did she really think he was interested in her sister's address in Roxmere or her own address in London? Still, he couldn't help glancing over and seeing that her name was Elsie Ferris. Then his own name was called. Julian was running down the platform, pushing past people and calling out, and explaining about not being able to find a parking place.

'Thanks so much for waiting with him,' Julian said to Mrs Ferris.

'She wasn't waiting with me,' corrected Henry crossly.

Mrs Ferris only smiled up at Julian. Then she added another telephone number to the note.

'You must excuse us rushing off like this,' Julian panted, 'but I'm on a yellow line!'

She held out the envelope but Julian was already hurrying away and Henry, loaded down with his bags, hadn't got a free hand. He looked back once and saw her, with the envelope still in her hand, rejoining her sister.

He would have waved, if he'd had a free hand.

The sports car was parked on a double yellow line with its engine running noisily. The keys were in the ignition. Julian jumped in and swept a mess of papers and polythene bags and crumbs from the passenger seat. Henry got in too and was aware that several people – mostly women – were watching them.

Julian seemed more like an artist than an uncle. Other people's uncles were older and fatter and interested in sport and DIY. Adam's uncle, the one who was a bank manager, always wore a tie, even at weekends, and they joked that he probably wore it in bed. Julian wasn't like that. He was tall and thin, with long hair held back in a coloured band. He wore a pink T-shirt and trousers that looked like cut up curtains. No wonder people stared.

Henry's sister Rose thought that Julian was good-looking. Henry had overheard her talking to a friend the last time Julian had stayed with them. It had seemed a really odd thing to say about one's uncle, but her friend had agreed, especially about his eyes. Julian had blue eyes, like the rest of the Constable family, but his were lighter. They were chalky blue and so striking that you looked at his face again, to make sure.

Henry settled his feet among the rubbish with an enormous sense of relief. The suburban world of car vacuums and air-fresheners seemed far, far away as Julian roared along the main street and through the amber lights.

'I didn't think you'd come,' he shouted, above the engine.

'My parents didn't want me to, but I did.'

'Good for you,' said Julian. The words were snatched from his lips by the wind. They were driving very fast.

Henry leant back: if this was unsuitability, he liked it. They were beginning to climb the hill. At the top, just before the brow, lay the walls of Roxmere Park. He finally saw glimpses of them among the foliage, and his faint memories sharpened. On the top of the hill the land would fall away to the sea.

'Why?' shouted Julian. 'Why did you want to come?'

'I don't know.' Now poised for its descent, the sudden, slanting brilliance of the sun on the sea dazzled Henry. He shielded his eyes. 'I get so bored at home.'

Julian changed down carelessly and the gears grated.

'Well, there's not much to do here. Not now. You did know that the park was closed down years ago?'

'Yes.'

'So there's not much to do!'

'I don't like doing much.'

'Don't you!' Julian laughed. 'I thought you city Constables were always busy. Whenever I've stayed with you, you were always dashing off all over the place. Music and sport, wasn't it? You're not the runner then?'

'No. That's Ed. They say he's got talent.'

'Good for Ed.'

He had slowed the car down and then turned off the main road so suddenly that both Henry and the rubbish around his feet were tossed to the side of the car. He gripped the seat.

'So is music your thing?'

'No. That's Rose and Tom. He's the one with the band.

It's a group really, I mean it's going to be a group. Actually – ' he was about to mention Ali Draper but Julian had stopped the car and got out.

He unlocked a wooden gate which was set into the boundary wall. It looked too narrow for the car, but they just managed it, with the ivy and brambles trailing down and catching against the metal as though they would have held it and then torn it to ribbons, if they could.

Julian locked the gate, and Henry, turning round to watch him, shivered. On this side of the wall the trees grew so thickly that they held off the sun.

'I don't remember this at all.'

'You wouldn't,' grinned Julian. 'This part was never opened to the public. My father wanted it kept private.' Julian's eyes were blue, blue as pale chalk, there in the dark, close wood.

It wasn't really a road at all: just a way between the trees, with the wheels sinking into the rustling, scaly skin of fallen leaves. Occasionally the sun flashed through, but nothing else stirred.

'Aren't there any animals at all?' asked Henry, still gripping the seat, though the car barely moved.

'Yes. There are a few: old favourites, of course. And old enemies that Father couldn't find homes for.'

'But they don't come down here, into this wood?'

'I don't know.' Ahead, they could see where the shadows ended. 'I'm not really interested in the animals.' Julian shrugged. 'Father still is, of course, but I'm sure he'll tell you all about it. He's expecting great things from you. He has decided that you will have the makings of a naturalist.'

Then they were out of the wood and back on the tarmac road that ran through the park. The sun streamed down on Henry's head and shoulders and there, before them, was the house. Henry didn't know if it was really old, but it was certainly large. It was built of dark red brick, and its dark, empty windows were edged with grey stone. No curtains blew in the breeze and no door stood open to let in the warmth. A great sweep of bright gravel lay before it so that Henry was reminded of a heavy boat beached upon a bank of shingle far from the touch of the sea.

Beyond the drive was a terrace with a low wall covered with honeysuckle and a few steps leading down to grass. There, under the cedar tree, something moved when they slammed the car doors. It was a small group of wildebeest. They turned and scattered, then came together and wheeled around and settled further away. There they stood, nodding and shifting and swinging their heavy, bearded heads as they watched with uncertain eyes. As Henry turned towards the house he smelt the trampled dusty places where their bodies had been, under the black-branched cedar.

No one came to meet them. Julian called out to his father, then looked into a couple of rooms while Henry waited in the empty stone hall. Sunlight fell through the windows in neat blocks of light and somewhere, unseen, a clock ticked. Julian went to the foot of the stairs and shouted. His voice echoed, but was not returned.

'I'm sure he'll be down in a moment.'

Henry stood in the middle of the hall with his case still in his hand.

'He won't have forgotten, not my father. He'll be busy with something.' Julian glanced at his watch.

Henry could feel the coldness of the hidden earth beneath the great stone slabs. An official notice-board still asked visitors to Kindly Inquire at Reception but the painted arrow pointed to a window that had long been boarded up.

'I'm frightfully sorry about this.' Julian looked at his watch again.

'It doesn't matter.'

It would be tea time at home. They would be eating in the garden on such a lovely afternoon and his mother would have made something special to celebrate the athletics meeting, maybe ice-cream. She was famous for it. His father would be leaning forward in his deck-chair, reaching for some more and saying that her ice-cream was better than bought, miles better. He always said that, and then grumbled quietly about the neighbours and their noise. Alison Draper would be lying out in the full sun with only a couple of scarves spread over her – and not always that, the twins said. They had seen her. She could lie there for hours, listening to the same music over and over again, and doing nothing at all.

'Father?' Julian went through a passage to the back of the house and Henry followed awkwardly with the case. There was no one in the kitchen and, even more strangely, little sign of life at all: no kettle or mug by the sink, no bread board with crumbs and the end of a loaf. It didn't even smell of food, but of something old and rotten.

'I'm so sorry,' said Julian. 'I mean, I can wait . . .'

'You don't have to wait.' Henry went back into the hall. At least it was sunny there. 'I don't mind waiting alone.'

'Don't you?' Julian was clearly relieved. 'It really is too bad of him. After inviting you specially.'

Julian was making it all worse, hanging around and apologizing.

'Do you think I could phone? If it's convenient. Only my mother asked me to.' He didn't want Julian to imagine that he cared.

'Of course! What a good idea. Look, there it is.'

It was a very old-fashioned phone of fading black mica with a cloth-covered cord twisted and curled behind. The dial was stiff. Henry heard it ring and ring up there in their pretty, carpeted hallway which always smelt of pot-pourri and dried flowers. One of them would have to run in from the garden. 'Well, somebody get it, I'm eating,' his father would shout, and then his mother would be there, panting a bit from the hurry. She'd want to hear all about the journey and whether he'd enjoyed his sandwiches, and she'd tell him about athletics and about Ed's victories.

Only she didn't. Nobody answered the phone at all.

For a moment more he held the receiver away from his ear, listening to the sound of it calling in vain. Then he put it carefully back on the two forks of the stand. When he turned round Julian had gone.

He decided to study the pictures. They were photographs of the animals that Uncle Arthur had collected. There were two of lions on the cliffs overlooking the sea and one of wonderful pink flamingos on the lake. There was a close-up of a chimpanzee, an old mother with a torn ear and heavily ridged brow who looked up with a calm, gentle eye from the cradled head of her baby. There was a particularly beautiful one of zebra rearing up from something hidden among the flowers in the meadow.

Wherever could his family be? They must have gone out, without him, to celebrate Ed's success. It was most unfair.

Hung at the far end of the hall, facing the entrance, was an enlargement of the most well-known photograph of Arthur Constable. It was the one that was on the cover of his book about saving animals from extinction. They had the book at home, though he didn't know if anyone had read it.

The photo showed a small, scholarly man with thinning,

reddish hair and round, wire-framed spectacles. It was like Julian's face, but sharper, and with the mouth set and determined. Arthur Constable was sitting on a fallen log, writing in a notebook with a stub of pencil. Crouched in the foreground with an equally studious expression on his face was a chimpanzee. He was inspecting a small twig which he held at exactly the same angle as the pencil. It was a peaceful scene with an evening sun setting huge and crimson above a background of lush, tangled bushes. Tom always said that the photo must be a fake with bits added after, but his parents had disagreed. They said that Tom was just being negative and enjoyed criticizing everything. Uncle Arthur was respected, they said, and wouldn't have used a fake. Henry hadn't thought much of the photo when he saw it on the book, yet here, in the silent hall, it was beautiful.

Nevertheless, he was fed up. His uncle should have been at home, or his family should. Unless something had happened – an accident, say, at the track, and they'd had to go to Casualty with Ed. But they still should have phoned to see if he had arrived safely. Maybe they were waiting for the cheap rate after 6 p.m. – but it must be six by now.

He looked at his watch. It was only three. So the last race hadn't even started. It was as though time wouldn't pass, as though things had slowed up. He blinked and stepped up to the photograph. Now he saw details in the enlargement that he had previously thought to be only leaves and shadows. He put his case down and, peering very closely, saw the limbs of other creatures amongst the trees. There, around that branch, were fingers and a thumb, the sun just touching the clasping nails. Surely there, behind the leaves, there were eyes, which met his. He looked away and then back, and felt himself drawn on to seek out some figure that had been there that evening watching the watcher.

Holding his breath, Henry stretched up on his toes, intent on seeing clearly, on pushing the leaves aside.

A light touch on his neck made him cry out in fear. He stumbled over his case and fell flat on his back, grazing his elbows on the stone.

'It's a good job we aren't in the jungle now,' said a firm voice. 'There wouldn't have been an animal left for miles around.'

Arthur Constable leant down and held out his hand. It was fleshy and dry and it pulled Henry to his feet with surprising energy.

'It's a knack of mine,' said Arthur Constable. 'I'd never have seen anything if I hadn't learnt to move silently.' He pushed back his glasses and smiled at Henry. 'Come on then. Pick up that bag and I'll show you your room.'

He led the way up the stairs with remarkable speed for an old man, and Henry suddenly wondered how long his uncle had been in the empty hall.

Chapter 6

Henry was shown to a huge room in the middle of a long corridor. It was high as well as wide, and the wardrobe and chest of drawers were the size of garden sheds. Great, grey shutters hung above the window seat and when he pushed them back they moved reluctantly like the stiffly folding wings of some old, abandoned bird.

Yet he liked it. There was nothing of him here at all. He stuffed his few clothes into the drawers, and when he opened the heavy mirrored door of the wardrobe he saw that it was half full of clothes from some other age: women's dresses with the smells and colours of the past hung above a row of strange-shaped, unlikely shoes, and men's jackets hung on wire hangers like shed skins with all the bones drawn out. The colours had almost faded from the cushions in the window seat but years ago there had been flowers, he was sure, great, glowing bunches of soft petalled flowers. He thought of the other people who had sat here and gazed over the terrace, over the young green tips of the spreading cedar, to the distant glistening line of the sea.

It was wonderfully peaceful up in this room, with the sun streaming through the window and the rest of the great house held quiet and hidden behind the firm red bricks. Tomorrow he would explore: feel into the yellowed pockets of the clothes and lift up the coverings of tissue and brown paper. Then he could look more carefully at the collection of pots and bowls and masks which lined the corridor outside. He had the feeling that, after all, the visit was going to be all right.

Later, at supper, Uncle Arthur was all right too. When Henry had first responded to his uncle's call and hurried down to the kitchen he had been horrified. No saucepans bubbled on the stove nor was there any smell of gravy or crisping meat. He was starving. His sandwiches on the train seemed to belong to another century. His uncle took one look at his expression and laughed.

'Don't worry! You haven't got to live off air, or off the land, though you could. The land and sea around here provide everything you could want: fish, fowl, fruit – I bet a young fellow like you would have no trouble at all surviving.'

'I don't think I'd be very good at it.'

'Rubbish. You could learn. We can learn anything – if we're taught. Would you like me to teach you, Henry?'

'Yes. Yes, I would.' He wanted to look enthusiastic but his tummy rumbled treacherously.

'Well, Henry, luckily for you, I'm not only interested in preserving the old ways of life, I'm also interested in the latest in modern developments. You have to take advantage, Henry. That's my motto: take advantage to survive. Now sit down there,' he pointed to the end of the table where two knives and forks were laid. 'Sit down and count to thirty – no, thirty-four. And . . .'

Uncle Arthur put on a pair of pink oven gloves, and when a shrill little bell pinged somewhere just out of sight he laughed and took two sizzling dishes from a microwave. It was lamb curry and saffron rice with real Indian chutneys set out in little hollows on the plastic plates, like dabs of colours on an artist's palette.

'Wow!' Henry was impressed. It had that delicious restaurant taste. He always secretly regretted that Mrs Constable never served them what she called 'artificial food'. After the first course Uncle Arthur defrosted two enormous slices of chocolate gâteau. Again, it was wonderful, but rather heavy going after curry. While Henry ploughed on, his uncle talked about domestic slavery.

'I think I've solved it,' he said, licking his lips. 'I've reduced my slavery time to fifty-six minutes a week. Not bad, eh? That's just eight minutes a day. It used to be seventy, but I've knocked fourteen minutes off by learning the cooking instructions by heart.'

'But how do you know what each packet will say?'

'Black magic.'

Henry grinned, as he supposed it was a joke. One third of his gâteau still lay untouched.

'And don't you laugh too soon, my lad. There's more to black magic than people think. But in this case, it's not magic, it's experience: I always eat the same things. Every Monday the grocer delivers the same order.'

'Exactly the same?'

'Exactly. Monday lunch is cauliflower cheese and supper is pizza and trifle. Now don't look so astonished, Henry. Finish up. I don't like waste.'

'No.' He took another mouthful, although the thought of eating fifty-two helpings of curry and chocolate gâteau had suddenly taken his appetite away.

His uncle watched him scrape his plate clean and in the silence that followed Henry thought he heard something outside. Something out there called – and called again. For a moment his uncle looked anxiously from his plate to the darkening sky and he pushed his spectacles back up his nose. Henry swallowed and something softly touched – but did not scatter – the gravel that lay there, all around the house.

It wasn't fear that made Henry yawn. It was exhaustion and then the huge meal. He yawned again and again so that his eyes watered, and he gulped down some water, but the sweetness stuck to the roof of his mouth. His uncle had resumed his speech about freedom from domestic slavery.

'Especially women,' he was saying with a superior smile. 'I'm afraid it's often grumble, grumble, grumble, with them! I don't believe that women really want to be free of domestic work. If they did, they'd take advantage, like me! Nobody has to slave in the kitchen nowadays. But they do.'

Henry yawned and thought of his mother. She slaved: that ice-cream took hours, and sometimes if he woke in the night he heard her downstairs, still doing things in the kitchen.

'My mother grumbles. But not much.' He yawned again.

'Now Henry, don't think for one moment that I'm criticizing your dear mother. I'm sure she does her best. It's just that the fact of the matter is, most people don't want to be free. Oh dear,' his uncle got up and laid a hand on his shoulder. 'I haven't offended you, have I, Henry?'

'No.' He felt a little awkward. 'I think you're right, actually. It is like that at home.' His uncle patted him approvingly. 'I mean Mum is always grumbling about what a lot she has to do – but she doesn't really have to do it.'

They had left the kitchen now and were in the hall, at the bottom of the stairs. Henry felt another huge yawn coming on.

'And she does keep on about things, like the burglary that I told you about.'

His uncle nodded sympathetically.

'That really wasn't my fault, Uncle Arthur.'

'Of course it wasn't. And I'm sure nobody thought it was.'

Henry would have protested if another yawn had not rolled in and submerged him.

'Goodness me – what am I thinking of? Here's you, asleep on your feet, old man, and me still carrying on. But thanks for listening. It's good to have an intelligent audience for a change: I've faith in you, Henry. Now – straight to bed, or your mother'll have something else to grumble about! I'll take you on the "Grand Tour" tomorrow, eh?'

Henry was half-way up the stairs when his uncle, who was staring intently at his younger self in the famous photograph, called out to him.

'Now don't you worry about anything while you're here, Henry, because I think you might be like me and discover that most things are the fault of other people! So off you go, and sleep well.'

But Henry didn't. He woke a dozen times in a night of anxious dreams during which something pawed at the moonlit gravel and turned up things that made him gasp and sweat.

He finally broke free from sleep and was instantly and unexpectedly delighted not to be at home. He had not closed the shutters and now the sun streamed in. The park looked wonderful. He dressed quickly and then pushed up the window and leant out. The wildebeest were back under the cedar tree, and coming towards them was a small group of five or six chimpanzees. One, who must have been a youngster, gambolled on all fours, but the others walked upright.

It was so beautiful. He leant further out and felt the warmth on his face and shoulders. Below, on the terrace, there were more of the huge earthenware pots that lined the corridor, but these had been filled with flowers – roses, geraniums and daisies – which tumbled and sprawled in the sunlight, their petals warming then falling on to the gravel. Henry could have watched it all for ever and ever.

The troupe of chimpanzees continued its way towards the house. Now there appeared to be eight or nine of them, though it was hard to count at a distance. He could only see that the one in front was enormous. They skirted the wildebeest but disturbed a group of black-headed gulls which flew up screaming and wheeling. They climbed the steps to the terrace and then some seemed to hang back while others rushed forward making excited hooting and panting noises. Leaning out further, he saw that the ones at the front were feeding from huge bunches of bananas. The young one tried to grab some but was frightened back by its elders.

Then he heard his uncle shouting. 'Haven't I told you to keep away? Don't you understand that they can be dangerous?'

Someone replied lightly and laughed, and it could not have been the answer that was expected because Uncle Arthur went on, even more furiously: 'Then you must be even more stupid than you look!'

Henry heard quick steps across the gravel.

'*And* shut that door properly!'

A latch was lifted and a door swung open and slammed shut.

As his uncle came into view below, Henry eased himself back behind the shutters and let out the great chestful of breath that he had been holding in.

When his uncle sat down on one of the low terrace walls a couple of chimpanzees came up to him. He brought out some titbit and Henry watched the animals take it with their long, strong fingers reaching trustingly and delicately into the soft, upturned palm of the old man.

He couldn't blame his uncle for shouting. It was

probably some local kid who had come into the park for a dare. Henry had thought that all those fences were needed to keep the animals in. Now he realized that they might be needed to keep the people out. Maybe some idiots teased or harmed the animals. And of course, the animals were wild, or had been. He needed to ask his uncle about that, just to make sure. It wasn't that he was afraid or anything. He just wanted to be sure.

He'd promised his parents to ask about that too . . .

Then he smelt the bacon. Someone was frying bacon, and for a second his teeth bit into the hot, crisp fat and he was terribly hungry. He combed his hair quickly. He could imagine it all: with fried bread and mushrooms on the plate too. He'd phone home after breakfast, absolutely definitely, though he was unwilling to keep his uncle waiting after witnessing his quick temper.

Oddly, the kitchen didn't smell of bacon. It was still and cold and actually smelt of damp dishcloths and yesterday's curry. Henry couldn't even see a kettle so he ran the tap in the sink and drank awkwardly from the stream of water. It tasted odd and sweet and curled down his chin and neck on to his shirt and made him shiver. Perhaps he had imagined the bacon, like travellers imagine oases of palm trees in the empty desert. It was not as if the Constables had big fry-ups at home and he was missing them. It was just . . . odd. Anyway, his appetite had gone now.

Back home they would have all finished breakfast and gone out, except his mother. She'd be there, tidying away, getting ready for Sunday lunch. If he phoned now he'd catch her alone. She'd be really pleased. He only wanted a quick word – though he told himself he didn't even want that. He went back into the hall and dialled the first three digits, then stopped. It sounded too loud, especially when he didn't know for sure where his uncle was. He carefully replaced the receiver, and looked over his shoulder. No one was there. Only the figures in the picture held their steady gaze under the dappled forest light.

He ran upstairs to his room, flung himself down on the bed and almost cried, which was absolutely and unbelievably stupid since he hadn't cried for years and years. And anyway – nothing was wrong.

Chapter 7

Then he heard it again. Right outside his door the same light voice – a girl's voice, he realized now – said, amidst the same soft laughter:

'Silly old fool! I wasn't doing any harm!'

'Stella – you must be more careful.' This reply was in an older, more cautious voice.

He slipped from the bed and crept over to listen at the door.

'Careful? I'm always careful!' The girl laughed with more abandon. 'Just watch how careful I am, Mum!'

'Please, Stella . . .'

He could hear them, laughing together, a girl and her mother, he was sure, laughing over nothing at all, like they did at his home. It was odd that Uncle Arthur hadn't mentioned them.

Then something crashed down outside. It smashed into bits and ended their laughter like a thread cut. There was silence. Then, like conspirators, he heard them scrabbling around on the floor, gathering up the evidence.

He wanted to go and help, to let them know, at least, that he was there, but he couldn't. He just stood stupidly behind the door which separated them.

'There are some bits missing!'

'Then find them! Quickly!'

There was no laughter in their voices now, and he heard their fingers searching across the dark, dusty boards.

Looking down, he saw one of the missing bits. It was a fragment of earthenware with a pattern of black dots: he recognized it as part of a large bowl from the corridor outside.

Silently, this girl, this 'Stella', reached under his door. It could only have been a girl, with a wrist so thin and knobbly rings all over little fingers with bitten nails. She was almost touching the piece that lay there, beside his feet. She was stretching out those little white hands and Henry, meaning to help, nudged it to within her grasp.

She gasped and ripped back her arm so that it must have hurt her, but straightaway she flung open the door to reveal Henry still standing there with the broken bit between them.

'You creep!' she cried. 'What do you think you're playing at?'

She was wild, but the older woman behind her smiled apologetically at Henry and shrugged.

'You scared the life out of me!' Stella hissed, with her ringed hands held up to her white face.

'I didn't mean to. I thought you needed that bit.'

'Well I don't. I don't need any of it!'

Yet she didn't look like a person who scared easily, not with that red hair. It was hair as red as paint, not naturally red, but the colour of ripe cherries or old-fashioned roses, and it was as short and fluffy as a cat's.

'I'll help,' he said, but helplessly.

'Go on then.' She thrust the dustpan full of bits at him but Henry stepped back and between them they dropped it and the fragments ended up all over the floor.

'Everything all right up there?' It was his uncle calling from below.

'Yes, Mr Constable! Sorry about the noise.' The woman

58

had hurried to the top of the stairs. 'I just dropped my bucket of cleaning things.'

'So long as no harm's done.'

'No,' she answered, 'no harm's done.'

'Glad to hear it, Mrs Elder. Now while you're up there, would you knock on the guest-room door and see if my great-nephew is ever going to get up?'

'Certainly.' She avoided looking at Henry and knocked all the same.

The girl Stella crouched on the floor and silently picked the pieces up one by one. He really would have helped had not Mrs Elder called out that he was just on his way down. There was nothing for it: Henry had to step over the girl, moving with horror in case he touched that awful hair.

Downstairs his uncle was pleased to see him and asked if he'd slept well. It was, he said, the perfect morning for a tour of the park. As they made their way to the Land-Rover his uncle remarked:

'Your parents called last night, after you'd gone to bed. After *I'd* gone to bed, actually.'

Henry's stomach tightened.

'I had to get up to answer it, but I told them that everything was fine. That was what you would have said, wasn't it, Henry?'

'Oh yes.'

'Well that's a good thing. I thought you'd agree with me.' He chuckled.

Henry smiled too, and as he climbed into the Land-Rover he experienced that odd, lightheaded feeling that follows hunger.

The tour of the park was wonderful. Within its high walls and wire fences they saw wildebeest, zebra and chimpanzees, deer, parrots, lions and unfamiliar cattle, pink

59

flamingos, monkeys and more; more than he could remember, and it was all so cleverly arranged. The many fences were so well camouflaged that it seemed as though the animals really roamed freely. It was even better than Henry had anticipated.

On the lake the outrageous flamingos looped back their necks and watched the neat ducks dive and splash amongst the water lilies. A swan with eager, paddling cygnets arched her wings and glided to the far shore where zebra briefly drank. It was magical. Deer leapt and grazed and ran through meadows where white daisies grew among sudden scatterings of crimson poppies. And up above, clouds billowed in a windy seaside sky.

Henry was enthralled. His uncle spoke of the animals with unexpected affection and passion, and he remembered what his teacher Mrs Silk had said. At the edge of the hazel wood they glimpsed the band of chimpanzees. His uncle pointed out the nests which the animals had built by bending over and intertwining the branches. This, he explained, was where the chimpanzees slept at night. He also pointed out the remains of a rabbit. There wasn't that much left – a bit of fluff, a gobbet of chewed skin and bone, and a bit of a paw caught on brambles.

'It could have been something else – a fox, perhaps – but chimps are carnivorous,' said Uncle Arthur. 'They enjoy a bit of meat and will kill for it, sometimes.'

He revved up the engine to get the Land-Rover over a muddy patch and, once out in the sunlight, reminded Henry to be careful, particularly in the woods.

'Because of the chimps?'

'Those too. But really because of the snakes.'

'Snakes?'

'Adders mainly. It's the fault of the mild winters we've

had – the population has exploded!' His uncle laughed, then lowered his voice. 'Not just adders, Henry. There's a couple of tropical breeds – not that their bite is fatal, not unless you're extra sensitive – I hadn't expected them to breed, to adapt to our climate so well, but they are really flourishing.'

Henry glanced at his uncle in horror, but the old man was watching the track ahead and didn't notice.

'I wouldn't have mentioned it, but I know that you're not the sort of person to gossip about this. Like I said, the snakes aren't that dangerous, and anyway they are contained within the wood, but you know how stupid people are. People are such fools: they'll panic at nothing at all. But you're not a fool, are you, Henry?'

'No.' He was feeling sick and was glad that his uncle hadn't looked at him.

'I knew you were the sensible one. Julian always said that you were the best of the bunch in your family. But take care all the same.'

'Yes.' Henry was flabbergasted.

It was only later, when his legs began to ache, that he realized that he had lifted his feet off the floor of the car and was holding them there, rigid in mid-air.

The large wild cats were behind a mesh fence that followed the curve of the River Rox. This broad sweep of water made the ideal natural boundary, though naturally, his uncle explained, he had also put the high barrier. There were now only three lions left: an aged male and two smaller females.

'They're as tame as kittens, usually,' said his uncle, operating the beam which opened the first of two gates by remote control. One lioness strolled over to meet them. The others hung back. Uncle Arthur turned off the engine and got down. He moved slowly. So did she. She passed and repassed him, so closely that her head brushed his sleeve. Henry could hardly bear to watch. The other lioness came over, though the old male only watched with drooping, matted head from the centre of the track. Then one of the females gently nudged the man and he stumbled back against the bonnet, only just keeping on his feet. Finally both animals moved round to the back and stood up against the tailboard, making the whole vehicle rock.

'Nothing today, ladies!' laughed Uncle Arthur, climbing back in. He eased the vehicle forwards towards the old male, who swung his head but did not move from their path.

'They were hoping it was feeding time. They know that I always carry the carcasses in the back there.'

Henry looked round and now saw some bloodstained sacks and chips of bone and other bits that had stuck here and there. The old lion still stood before them with swaying head and eyes of golden beauty and, it now seemed, of sadness. At the very last minute Uncle Arthur swung the wheel and avoided him.

A further set of gates on the far side of the enclosure brought them on to a cliff-top path and Henry realized that the photograph of the lions which hung in the hall must have been taken from up there. The chalk cliffs formed another natural boundary, for they dropped down a couple of hundred feet to the shore and were unscalable. The fence must have been put in after the photo was taken. His uncle drew up so that they could admire the view. Henry heard the waves rolling in and running up over the sand to break against the softened white rocks.

Then he thought he heard something else. Some other rhythm beat in on the breeze, and didn't ebb, but beat on, though his uncle didn't notice it. Instead Uncle Arthur started up the engine and said with sudden loud irritation:

'I'm afraid there's something I have to mention, while we're out here.' He had begun to drive very fast along the bumpy track. Henry noticed with horror how close they were to the edge.

'If it's about the animals, honestly, I'll be really careful.' Henry was holding on now, tightly. 'Mother and Father warned me, actually.'

'Did they now?'

'Yes . . . but . . .' He sensed in a moment of tight silence that he had said the wrong thing: he'd tried to be too clever, probably. 'But of course, they didn't mention the snakes. And you needn't worry, Uncle Arthur. I won't go down there again.'

'Again?' The old voice had sharpened so that it cut right through him.

'Ye – es. Uncle Julian drove me through there yesterday!'

'Did he now?'

'Only we didn't get out, or stop. So you needn't worry.'

'Needn't I?'

Henry didn't know what to say. His uncle drove on, tight-lipped, his face contorted with some inexplicable anger. He tried, in the grim silence, to see his uncle's point of view. After all, Julian must have known about the snakes in the wood, yet had deliberately gone there. It did seem irresponsible. Supposing the car had broken down?

Then his uncle laughed. He threw back his head and laughed and clapped his hands up and down on the steering wheel and had to push his glasses back up his nose. Henry was so relieved to have that huge weight of bad temper removed that he would have done anything, almost, for his uncle. He felt truly grateful, as though he had been forgiven.

'You see, that's just it!' roared Uncle Arthur. 'That's exactly what I was trying to talk to you about. And you, dear boy, with your special understanding, you have made it easier for me. Henry Constable, I *knew* you were different. I knew it from the moment I heard your voice on the phone when you accepted my invitation. Why, your brother and sister never even bothered to reply to my letters.'

Although it was nice to hear all this, Henry half wished that his uncle would change the subject. He pushed his face into a grin and noticed with relief that they were heading home.

'As you so cleverly understood, Henry, it's my son Julian that I wanted to talk to you about.'

Henry kept quiet. It seemed safest.

'He and I don't exactly see eye to eye . . . It's just because he's an artist: the artistic temperament is difficult, and always has been. Everybody knows that. Whereas scientists like myself – well, we deal in facts, don't we, Henry?'

'Yes.'

'With us, what you see is what you get, eh Henry?'

'Oh yes.'

'Whereas artists – well, they change things, don't they? Distort them even. So just remember, Henry, while you stay in Roxmere Park you are *my* guest. You do what I want – not that I shall want anything, much. We scientists and naturalists are simple fellows at heart. Simple and straightforward. You follow me, don't you?

'Oh yes.'

'Good. I knew you would, Henry.'

The wheels bit deeply into the gravel.

'So don't take any notice of old Julian,' Uncle Arthur smiled. 'He has ideas, dangerous ideas – you know what artists are like. They don't mean to make trouble, it's just the way they are. So, Henry, you mustn't take any notice of him, if he says anything, or tells you anything. Eh, Henry?'

Henry was going to ask what he meant, but didn't. Instead he heard himself yapping on about how his own father was having problems with his elder brother Tom, who was 'going through a phase' and was really cynical about everything 'on purpose', his father said. Henry couldn't stop himself. He followed his uncle up the steps as slavishly as a lap-dog, expecting at any moment that his uncle would silence him with an exasperated scowl, but he didn't. Uncle Arthur nodded instead. He actually nodded and smiled in a really sympathetic way. Henry was grateful for all this attention, though somehow something about it really puzzled him.

Later, when Henry went along the corridor to his room, he was surprised not to see any gap where the smashed bowl had been. He had meant to ask his uncle about the girl, but couldn't. Supper (fish curry and cheesecake) was over just as quickly as lunch (Irish stew and crème caramel) and Henry, who had always been a slow eater, didn't dare to stop and ask. Anyway, silence seemed safer, especially after that breakage.

He didn't ask about phoning home either: it was odd that, apart from talking about Tom and his father, he had hardly thought about his family at all. And it was obvious that they weren't missing him either.

That night, when he thought he was dreaming something totally idiotic about his mother and sisters, one of the figures in the landscape turned towards him, from behind an impossibly high fence, and he saw that she had red, red hair. He turned away from her so suddenly that he startled himself awake and heard a door opening, then shutting, downstairs. Then he was back inside the dream, and that girl was tearing at the fence, rattling it and shaking it, her purple mouth open and screaming. He reached out to touch her face but this time she turned away from him and he felt only the soft lines of her back.

Chapter 8

Soon Henry felt as though he'd been in the park for ever. It suited him and, to his surprise, he and his uncle got on together. There was a routine into which Henry fitted, and for the first time in years and years he wasn't bored. It was all the more remarkable because there wasn't anything much to do.

In the morning he joined his uncle on his regular tour of the park. Uncle Arthur, he discovered, got up very early, but Henry soon learned that the woman, Mrs Elder, came in every day to clean and wash up, and she was happy to set out a tray of breakfast things for him when he came down later. She was very quiet, not old really, but old-looking and worn out, with grey in her pulled-back hair and ugly old clothes: a loser, they'd have called her at school, and some would have said she was a slut. She and the girl Stella lived in one of the caravans in the field on the other side of the wall which bordered the far side of the terrace. The caravans used to be let to holiday-makers but now it seemed only two were occupied, one by Stella and her mother and the other by Julian. Henry hadn't been into the field yet. He sensed that his uncle wouldn't want him to.

He was learning to keep the accurate records which were essential, his uncle explained, for research. There were boxes to be ticked for animals identified and spaces for notes about anything unusual or interesting. It reminded Henry of school registration and he was beginning to appreciate the burden of responsibility that his uncle felt for keeping all the animals safely within the park.

Uncle Arthur was dedicated: all the risky tasks, like feeding the lions or administering medicines, he did himself. In the afternoons, when his uncle was in his study working on his new book, Henry was on his own. He didn't mind, indeed he liked it. Sometimes he did nothing at all but stretched out on his bed and closed his eyes. Before he slept he listened to the summer sounds of bees and soft-breasted wood pigeons and, from the distance, the roaring of lions. And sometimes he thought he heard the splash of the sparkling foam. Then he would sleep. When he came down later, rubbing his puffy eyes, with his face hot and red, his uncle never remarked that he'd 'wasted the best part of the day'. Henry appreciated that.

One afternoon, when it was really too hot to sleep, he wandered out on to the terrace and saw the girl, Stella. He saw her awful blob of hair first and quickened his pace. Then she did, too. He ran down a flight of steps and was sure he could cut her off, if she didn't trick him by escaping through the gate into the caravan field. It would be just like her to do something like that.

She stopped dead and turned right round to face him, and so caught him bent over and running, trying not to be seen.

'Did you want something?' she asked, coolly.

'No.' He must have looked really daft.

Now that they were face to face he didn't know why he'd bothered to follow her.

'I was going to look at the lions,' he muttered.

She was pale and thin with a face that wasn't like a school-girl's. Even Rose, whom everybody described as pretty, didn't look like this close up. This girl had skin like white velvet.

'OK,' she said, 'I'll go there, then.' She ran her hands through that hair.

'But you can't, because . . .'

'Because?' Her voice had lightened with laughter.

There wasn't any reason, or at least none that he could explain. It was just that he'd put on shorts, because it was so hot, and not decent shorts either. They were some horrid old things like cut-down trousers that you'd expect to see middle-aged men wearing on holiday. His mother must have put them in his case at the last moment. He couldn't walk beside her dressed like that, and with his legs all bare.

'Because?' she repeated.

'Because I'm going into the woods first.'

'So?'

She had already turned in that direction, just as if she didn't know about the snakes, or didn't care, which was more likely with hair like that.

'You can't come – not with those shoes.'

She was only wearing summer sandals and the two bands of plaited leather didn't cover her white feet at all. Her toe nails were painted as red as her hair.

If he'd been with people from school they would have all laughed at her, but on his own he just sweated. If he'd been with Adam, he'd have known what to say. Girls fancied Adam and went out with him, though he never talked about it afterwards.

The sun was so hot on his head and shoulders that he felt the sweat run down his spine. He probably smelt of it.

'Because of the brambles,' he said at last, hopelessly, guessing from her smile that she couldn't care less. And it was too late anyway.

He was already following her towards the woods, under

the high, relentless sun, and if he didn't trip over and break his ankle in the next minute they would both be stepping into that deceptive soft brown covering of dry leaves.

Maybe she did know about the snakes and maybe, unlike him, she just wasn't afraid.

She stopped suddenly, at the edge where the sunlight was dappled and the pink barbed hoops of wild rose reached back to the light.

'There,' she whispered, pointing.

'What?'

'There, under the tree.'

When he still couldn't see she put her cool hand on his arm and showed him, and the chill touch of those little, glittering rings made him jump.

One of the chimps was turning over the leaves at the base of a tree.

'It's Dodo, isn't it?' she asked.

Henry shrugged.

'Or is it Charles?'

He shrugged again, quite at a loss.

'Hasn't your uncle even told you their names yet?'

'He's very busy,' said Henry defensively. 'He's writing a new book.'

'Oh that,' she laughed, then added, 'Actually your uncle has forbidden me to go near the chimps.'

'Good! I mean, you won't go, will you?'

'No – but only because I promised my mum. Not because he told me. She's afraid of losing her job if I annoy him.'

'That's cleaning, isn't it?'

'Yes. It's good because we get the caravan rent-free.'

Henry would have hated admitting that his mother did cleaning, but this girl acted as though it were a job like any other.

'So we won't go into the woods.' He just wanted to be sure.

'We can still go,' she said, 'but not "near".' She was moving again, very slowly.

The chimp paused to watch them, then returned to its task.

'I'm sure that was Dodo. She's always looking for slugs and stuff.'

'Why?'

'To eat, of course. Doesn't your uncle tell you anything?'

'Of course he does. All sorts of things. I even help with his records.'

'Oh, those.'

'It's important. He says that good record-keeping is the basis of all research. If you don't know which animals have escaped—'

'Escaped? That's rubbish, they can't escape.'

'Yes they can.'

'How? How can they escape?'

'I don't know. That's what he said.' He was beginning to dislike her intensely.

'You don't know a thing, do you?' she muttered. 'Oh forget it. Come on.'

She had stepped into the wood and sank ankle deep in its leaves.

'Come on, Henry.'

But he couldn't and turned back. He couldn't be told what to do by some stupid girl with even stupider hair. He looked back once and saw that she had gone in deeper still. She would have been invisible were it not for that red hair.

Stupid cow. She had ruined the whole afternoon and it would serve her right if she did tread on a snake – not to be bitten, not really, but just to get a good scare. He kicked at a butterfly on a tussock of grass.

Now he didn't want to go and watch the lions. It was too

hot. In fact it was too hot to be outside at all. The old burden of boredom and irritation settled down on the back of his neck and clung on. He'd been happy until she had said all that, and now he was just fed up. No wonder his uncle had shouted at her.

He reclimbed the steps up to the house and his feet and shoulders ached as though he had been hauling loads uphill. If it hadn't been too much bother he'd have turned back and yelled the most horrible insults he could think of at her. His uncle was right. It *was* other people who were to blame. Anyway, you could tell she was dishonest from the way she'd broken that bowl and not owned up. She was as tricky as Ed and Em.

He glanced at his watch. It had stopped, but he guessed that it must be tea time, in other places. At home they'd all be there for Sunday tea – and his mother would have made scones to go with this year's strawberry jam. It was their Sunday treat – only perhaps it wasn't Sunday after all. Yet surely he'd been away for more than a week – and they hadn't phoned once. Apart from that first evening. It wasn't that he was homesick or wanted to speak to them particularly. He didn't. He wasn't missing them at all. It was only that he'd said he'd phone. So it was just a matter of keeping a promise, and now was a good time, since there was nothing else to do.

The hall was empty. Henry glanced around then picked up the receiver. He dialled quickly. His mother would be delighted. He looked over his shoulder as he listened to the unanswered ring. She'd be running in from the garden, or have her hands sticky from cooking. She'd be interested in the record-keeping.

'How dare you!' It was his uncle's voice, brutal and angry.

'I didn't,' gasped Henry, leaping round with his heart about to stop and the receiver thrust away behind him, as though he'd been caught shoplifting.

Then someone laughed.

'Don't be such an old fool! Do you really think I can be frightened off?' It was Julian.

Father and son were quarrelling in the kitchen – almost fighting maybe, because one of them banged his fist down on the table and their roars echoed through the house.

Henry wanted to escape. The kitchen door opened and he knew they were coming his way. Desperate as some cornered beast he looked frantically for a way out. Then, from behind him, but far, far away he heard his mother's voice.

'Hello? Jean Constable speaking. Hello? Hello?' He could hear her bewilderment.

He slowly raised his arm and began to say 'It's me,' but back up there, in the pretty, flowery hall, she turned to someone else and said impatiently 'It isn't anyone,' and put the phone down.

Henry raced up the stairs, two, three at a time. He didn't go into his room but ran along the corridor and up the next flight of stairs, then, still hearing their angry voices, fled up the last flight to the attic.

Below, they snapped and snarled, and he sat on the top step and shivered. He had never heard a quarrel like this. At home his mother wouldn't allow it. People blew their top at school but those rows usually stayed there, locked in with the crooked writing on the board and the soiled colours of lost games kit. He hugged his knees to his chin and was thankful that the sun fell in warm squares from the high, barred windows. Below, he heard Julian's mocking laughter. The front door was opened and then slammed shut with such violence that Henry thought he felt the rush of air on his face.

He leant against the banisters and heard a car sweeping off through the gravel. The house settled down but he couldn't, and sat as though paralysed by his own thumping heart. Nothing further stirred, yet he found that he was holding his breath, almost suffocating, and waiting. At long last a door opened and then it closed, a key turned and he knew that the other one had also gone on his way. Henry shut his eyes and tilted his head back and felt the stifling anxiety split and tear and fall away like an old tight skin.

In relief he stretched his legs out towards the sun, settled himself again and breathed in the old remembered scent of dust. As his cheek touched the warm boards, he felt the rustle of the leaves turned over by her feet.

The pain of the bite woke him and he jumped up, grabbing his leg where the snake had got him, and almost overbalanced down the stairs. The skin had been punctured, then torn, and there was a smear of blood below his knee where a jutting nail had gone in. He must have lain on top of it and never realized. He spat and rubbed away the blood. The house was still quiet but somehow he didn't want to go downstairs. Not yet. He shifted his position to avoid the nail and was glad he hadn't run up there with bare feet.

Unlike Stella. He should have tried to tell her, even if she had laughed at him. Then he remembered what his uncle had said about things usually being other people's fault. So he wouldn't feel too guilty about it: after all, those snakes hadn't been introduced into the hazel wood by him. Nevertheless, he would have been quite glad to have looked out of the window and seen her running back up the terrace steps.

He rubbed his eyes, which were sticky with sleep, and he remembered. He had sat on this same top step before. He had traced a pattern between the nail heads years ago. He had traced it in dust that had been as thick as fur. He'd stroked it, pushed it into little rolls and mounds and then lain down really close to see just what the dust was made of. Then he had seen the gap.

It was still there. He stretched his arm towards it, then waited, listening – which was idiotic, because he wasn't doing anything wrong. Slowly, he slid his fingers, then his hand, then his wrist under the door. His heart raced: if anyone came up the stairs, he'd be trapped.

A steady draught of old, dank air touched his face and cautiously, carefully he felt into the emptiness; but what he had touched as a little boy was gone. Shutting his eyes and ignoring his hammering pulse, he rammed his arm in past the elbow and, grabbing at what was not there, felt a broken edge slash the palm of his hand wide open.

He dragged his arm back, grazing the elbow and crying out, not with the pain of the cut but with the fear of it. A bloody line ran from his little finger to the base of his thumb and he cradled his hand to him, not daring to look too closely. He felt the blood trickle down his wrist.

If only he had been at home, it would have been all right. Even if his mother didn't care about him, she'd have cared about the cut.

Whimpering like a hit dog on an empty street, he fled down the stairs and out on to the bright terrace. Whatever had crouched in the attic all these years would not get him there. His mother would have looked after him, whereas here there was no one. Then he thought of Mrs Elder. At least she'd smiled that day. He struggled to open the door in the wall with his left hand and then ran to the only caravan with washing flapping outside.

'It's me,' he cried, knocking on the flimsy door with bloodstained knuckles.

Stella looked out of the window with her hair sticking up and an open book held before her face.

'I need your mother.'

'You should have stayed with me.' She was laughing at him behind that book, he was sure, but now he didn't care.

Stella opened the door for him and he unclenched his fist and felt the edges of the wound pull, but she didn't realize how badly he was hurt. She only turned the tap on for him and climbed back on to the bunk to continue reading. Washed clean, it wasn't much more than a scratch and he felt he had been rather foolish. It only hurt in one place where there was something stuck under the skin.

'Oh no,' she said, seeing it and becoming suddenly concerned.

It was a sliver of brown pottery. She bit her lip and put down the book.

'It's my fault,' she said miserably. 'I didn't think anyone else ever went up there.' She bent over his hand. 'You've been in the attic, haven't you?'

He nodded, though he didn't understand her concern. He was going to explain, but she was trying to get hold of the fragment with her bitten nails, and it hurt.

'I hid the remains up there – you know, the remains of that bowl I broke. I used my mum's key and hid them in the attic, because Mr Constable never goes up there. I didn't think anyone else would. I'm really sorry.'

'It doesn't matter.'

She looked up at him.

'It's not your fault,' he snapped, not really wanting to explain, and fortunately she didn't ask. She just looked very relieved and then, somehow, the bit finally came out of the cut and she opened the tap all the way so that the wound was washed quite clean.

When he stepped down into the field again the first fat jolting drops of summer rain were beginning to fall. From the gate he looked back towards the caravan. She couldn't wave with her arms full of washing and pegs, but she smiled as the rain darkened the brightness of her hair.

Chapter 9

It rained for the rest of that afternoon and on into the evening. At supper his uncle was pleased: the water level in the Rox had fallen dangerously low over the last weeks. In one place the stones of the river bed could be seen. Henry asked if the animals had suffered because of the drought, but his uncle shook his head.

'No. Security is my main worry,' he said. 'When the water is so shallow anyone could just wade across and get into the park.'

'Or get out,' agreed Henry, through lemon meringue pie.

'What do you mean, "get out"?' barked the old man suddenly.

'Nothing, Uncle. I just – said it.' Henry looked away and tried to suck off the sweet stuff that had stuck all over his teeth. 'I was only thinking about the snakes. You know, those foreign snakes in the wood. I mean, *they* might get out, mightn't they? Wriggle over the river bed and then find a gap in the wall . . .' He wanted to shut up but couldn't.

'What gap, Henry? Have you seen one?' His uncle was watching him closely.

'No.'

'Then what are you talking about?'

'Nothing, honestly, Uncle. I was just talking.'

'I see. Now Henry, you shouldn't "just talk". It makes trouble. The world is too full of people who just talk. They'll talk about any stupid idea that comes into their heads and

the next moment there are other people listening to them!'
He laughed scornfully. 'As though anything *could* get out.
You do understand what I mean, don't you, Henry?'

Henry nodded but kept his head down.

'That's good. I knew you would understand.' Uncle
Arthur was smiling now and drumming his fingers on the
table.

The atmosphere remained awkward all the same, and
Henry was relieved when a sudden roll of thunder made
them both look up. He muttered something about being
tired and was glad to go upstairs to his room. Someone had
left a window open at the end of the corridor and as Henry
passed two masks hanging there a steady, warm draught
made them swing gently to and fro.

Later that night great squalls of wind blew a turmoil of
rain and snapped off twigs and sent wet, crushed leaves
slapping and sticking against the windows. At first Henry
refastened the shutters and pulled the old silk eiderdown
right up over his face, but it didn't work. He still couldn't
sleep, or maybe he did, but too briefly. He was woken again
by the shutters banging repeatedly, as though something
out there was desperate to be let in. He opened his eyes
carefully, not wanting to disturb anything, but the whole
room was restless with a billow of curtain swooping out
and the shutters unbarred and swinging in the wind.

Out there the light of the full moon beat back the heavy,
turning clouds and flashed in and out of the room as the
shutters swung and crashed. He had sensed the light like a
hand over his face and now sat up, shivering. Then, dragging the eiderdown with him, he climbed on to the window
seat and crouched there, watching.

Henry never saw storms like this at home: up there, other
things always interfered. His mother would come in to

remind him that he had school in the morning, or Ed and Em would spoil it all by switching on the light. Anyway, there wasn't so much sky back up there. The press of streets full of people, with buildings and signs and lights, always crowded out this emptiness.

Odd drops of rain flicked in through the window and he licked them from his lips, pulled the eiderdown over his shoulders and scratched himself where the ends of feathers stuck in and irritated. Suddenly, when the lightning slanted again he saw one of the chimps out there, just beyond the shelter of the cedar tree.

In that moment, while the light lingered, he saw him reach up with outstretched arms and open hands, as though to gather up the shafts of rain or light. Yet, when Henry looked again, the figure was gone and the lightning fell into the black-topped cedar and scattered through its branches into the unseen earth.

He awoke so stiff and cold that he could scarcely move. His neck, where he had slept upright but bent against the window, hurt as though he had been shut up in a box. His hand throbbed and suddenly, painfully, he wanted to go back to a proper bed, but not this bed. He wanted to be in his own, boring room with the childish farmyard curtains and the sound of Tom's music annoyingly loud next door.

At home somebody would probably be up even at this early hour. Anyway, they'd have to get up if he phoned. If he slipped straight downstairs and phoned now, he'd probably get his mother and she'd be so pleased. She'd ask how he was. She'd say . . . that she was missing him. Surely that's what she would say, wouldn't she?

Yet somehow he knew that he daren't phone. He daren't risk it. He couldn't have borne to hear anything that wasn't pleasure in her voice, not this morning, not when his neck ached so miserably. He could always phone later on. Or tomorrow. Instead he made his way to the caravan park.

Stella was sitting on the steps, reading. She kept a finger on her place when she looked up and didn't ask about his hand, and he stood in the wet grass and was suddenly, ravenously hungry. Her plate, with bacon rinds and half a piece of toast, lay at her feet. Now he understood. That other morning the smell of fried bacon must have floated up from here. His mouth watered. He could have seized the toast and run off, like some starved dog, only he didn't, being him. Being him, Henry stood there, fingering the edge of the scratch and looking at the plate.

'Actually, there's some left,' she said, barely looking up. 'It's in the fridge under the blue shelf. You can cook it, if you want.'

'I don't,' he said, but could have killed for it, almost.

She shrugged and read on. Looking down he could see the fine gold line where the hair dye was growing out. It reminded him of flower petals, starting yellow and ending tipped with red.

'I saw one of the chimps last night.'

'Did you?'

'Yes. In the storm. It was standing all by itself near the cedar tree.'

'How odd.' She put the book aside.

'It wasn't odd: I expect it was enjoying the rain. I used to, when I was little. I stayed out once and got soaked and my mother was furious.'

'I can't imagine you doing that!'

He smiled awkwardly. She was right. Now it could almost have happened to some other little boy except that he could still remember how his cold shirt had stuck to his arms and his toes had slipped in the water inside his school shoes.

'But chimps,' she said, 'don't like the rain. Especially at night. Haven't you seen those nests that they make? They always stay in them at night.'

'Well, this one didn't.' He suspected that she disbelieved him. 'Maybe it was hurt, or ill, or something. But I did see it, honestly. Do you think I should tell my uncle?'

'No.'

She stood up and pushed the plate aside with her foot and said, to his utter horror, the laughter returning to her voice, 'No, don't bother him. *We'll* go and see if it's all right.'

'But I haven't had any breakfast.'

'Oh dear! Poor old Henry hasn't had his breakfast!'

To shut her up, he laughed too and followed as she walked purposefully off. But at least today she had proper shoes on.

He realized, as they approached the woods and chatted, that he would have to warn her. It wasn't just that he was scared. She wasn't that bad – at least, not as bad as she looked – so he ought to warn her. He decided that he wouldn't tell her about the snakes straight away because that would look cowardly, but as they stepped from the sparkling grass into the leafy, shaded wood his heart pounded dreadfully. She moved through the wood with ease while he stumbled and caught his clothes on brambles and didn't duck beneath the branches. Yet she hadn't grown up there. She told him that she and her mother had only come down from London a year ago. Mrs Elder had answered his uncle's advertisement for a housekeeper.

'But you like it?' suggested Henry.

'Mum likes it.'

'And you?'

'Yes. Yes, I like it.'

He knew that she wasn't telling the complete truth.

'Stella –'

'Ssh!' She laid that hand on him again, and pointed.

This time he pretended not to see, though the chimps were straight ahead. She tightened her grip on his arm. One of the animals was grooming another, absorbed in the intimacy, while the rest watched. Henry counted six of them and was sure that another was moving about amongst the bushes just out of sight. His uncle had told him that there were eight chimpanzees in all.

'Stella –'

She put her finger to her lips and very quickly and skilfully started to skirt right around the group and approach the animals which were in the undergrowth beyond. She was like some forest creature herself: a little deer maybe, or one of those darting parakeets from the jungles of South America. That was it, especially with her tantalizing red plume. From the way she moved and the smile on her face it did look as though she liked the park.

'Stella – please, Stella!'

Finally she stopped and turned to him and brushed aside the spray of green leaves that lay across her white neck.

'My uncle said –'

'It's all right, Henry. I *won't* go near them. I promised and I haven't forgotten.'

'It's not that. It's the snakes, Stella. Honestly, I should have told you before. I was going to, yesterday. It's the new snakes . . . from abroad, the ones that have bred so fast . . .'

'What snakes?' She didn't sound afraid but she looked around and stood quite still.

'I don't know what they're called but Uncle Arthur brought them in from abroad and now there are dozens of them.'

83

'Where?' Her glance had quickened.

'Here. In this wood.'

'Are you sure?'

'Yes. It's what he said. Haven't you ever seen one?'

She shook her head and shivered. Behind them the chimps were moving away, but neither of them stirred.

'And . . . and my uncle never warned you?'

She shook her head again and, putting her hand to her mouth, bit sharply along her nails.

'He said they couldn't kill you.'

She rolled her eyes.

'Not usually, anyway.'

'Great!' she said, suddenly coming back to life. 'That's just great, that is. The rotten old man!'

'I expect he forgot. Or thought you knew.'

'Do you really believe that?'

'Yes,' he said uncomfortably.

'Well,' she replied, 'maybe you do, so maybe you're a nicer person than I am. But I'll tell you something, Henry Constable, your Uncle Arthur stinks!'

'He doesn't. He's just . . . just . . .'

'Just what?'

'I don't know.'

'You can say that again. You don't know anything!'

She walked off and this time Henry felt that, somehow, she might be right. He followed her unhappily and was so preoccupied with thinking about his uncle that he had forgotten about the snakes, until she screamed.

She had gone on ahead and wasn't even trying to be quiet, but stamped and kicked her way along. When she cried out she was out of sight behind the bushes where the other chimps had been. Now something had happened to her.

How could his uncle have kept quiet and not warned

her? And anyway Henry didn't know what to do for snake bites, not really, though he'd seen someone in a film cutting an oozing red line into one with a razor blade. He couldn't do that to her, even if he'd had a blade.

She was on her hands and knees, but not crying; in fact she wasn't hurt at all. She was looking at something, there in the mud. The bushes edged a small clearing over which last night's rain-water must have gushed down from the higher ground on its way to the river. There in the sweep of fine, strewn mud was the print of a foot. There, a step further on, was half another print where the walker had stepped towards the grass.

In an odd way he felt cheated, until he saw that she really was upset by something.

'Someone has walked this way,' she said quietly.

'The other chimp was here. We saw it – well, we almost saw it, behind the bushes.'

'But this isn't a chimpanzee print.'

'It must be – I mean, *they* don't wear shoes.'

'It isn't, Henry. Their feet aren't like that – they've got much longer toes – and bigger feet altogether.'

'This is a little one.'

'It isn't, Henry. A human foot made this print.'

'All right then, so it did. What's the matter?'

'But *who* made it, and so recently? Did you? Did your uncle?'

'How do I know? Somebody must have. Somebody got in and walked barefoot after the storm. Maybe Julian did. Uncle Arthur says he's difficult. So maybe he came up here after the storm. Ran around without any shoes on. You know how daft artists are.'

'But Julian wouldn't do that – not if he knew about the snakes,' she said.

'He might. Uncle Arthur says he's irresponsible.'

'And you believe your uncle? Like you believe him about the snakes?'

'Yes! Don't you?'

She didn't answer, but pulled off her shoe and pressed her right foot into the mud beside the print. It was the same, though not exactly. Her foot was just smaller and more slender, a girl's foot. Looking at them, side by side, Henry felt a rush of giddiness and exhaustion. He didn't know what he thought, not about anything, any longer. He was only aware of his overwhelming hunger.

'Could I still cook that bacon?' he asked, and Stella nodded as she put on her shoe. They made their way out of the wood and back to the caravan in almost total silence.

Chapter 10

The storm was followed by several days of brilliant sun. It was hotter than ever and some of the animals were clearly troubled by this and by the growing clouds of insects. The old lion looked particularly miserable. The flies had settled on a sore patch around one eye and he tossed his head continually but was too feeble to dislodge them. Uncle Arthur noted this down in his records and talked of bringing in a vet.

While his creatures suffered in the heat, Arthur Constable flourished. He said that it reminded him of Africa, and made him feel young again, and Henry could not but admire the vigour and toughness of the old man. Now, after the daily tour was completed, he dropped Henry back at the house, and then returned to the park on foot to continue his work under the blistering sun. His observations would form a vital part of the book which he had been working on for the last ten years. When it was finally published it would definitely justify his ideas about the world and its animals, he said.

In the afternoons, while his uncle continued his work in his study, Henry usually went down to the caravans to look for Stella. For some reason they both avoided talking about the wood and didn't even mention the snakes or the footprints. If they talked about anything at all, it was of school and friends, but usually she would continue reading and he would do nothing at all. He didn't want to talk about home either. He didn't want to drag it into his new life in the park.

Then one evening, when they had gone past the lions' enclosure and were sitting beside the cliff path, looking out to sea, she closed her book and said:

'It isn't true!'

Henry looked at her and somehow guessed what she would say.

'There *aren't* any dangerous snakes in that wood, are there?' She was telling him, not asking. 'There aren't any, because *he* goes in there.' She was talking about his uncle. 'I've seen him, lots of times. And he's so careful about everything else. He just wouldn't take risks like that,' she said firmly.

Henry picked a handful of grass and began to unfurl it meticulously.

'There is something else, isn't there?' she persisted. 'There must be. There's something else in those woods.'

'Something else?' he echoed and knew that he had heard those words before. When he tried to remember, to think back, it was like returning to another country along ways that are unmarked. He rolled on to his stomach so he was close to the grassy edge, and listened to the waves running over the shingle below. Then, with difficulty, he began to retrace his steps. It seemed, under that hot sky, as though he would not find his way at all. His parents and brothers and sisters, Adam and Ali Draper, Pig Rory and Mrs Silk, even all that trouble with the burglary, it just didn't seem important now. It was as though the world within Roxmere Park had taken him over and the ebb and flow of these currents had dissolved away almost all the traces of his other self.

It was very hot and the light was very bright.

He put out his hand and touched her hair, but so gently that she might not have noticed. As he looked at her he saw that the collar of her shirt was worn through and frayed. Then he remembered: 'There are other things up there in the woods.' He *had* heard it before: Mrs Ferris had spoken those words in the train on the journey down. He also remembered how rude he had been in not saying goodbye, when he could have, so easily. He thought of the parting from his parents at the station and how he had longed for them to go so that he could be free. Then painfully he recalled what he had overheard that other hot night and he snatched back his hand as though he had been hurt again and the wound opened up.

Stella turned over on to her back and closed her eyes against the sun and he watched her settle herself into the grass amongst the rustling harebells and the papery pinks of fading thrift.

'People in the village,' she breathed, 'people in Roxmere, talk about this place.'

'Why?'

'They talk about it being all shut up.'

'So?'

'They say that it's all shut up because your uncle doesn't want people to know what he does up here.'

'That's stupid. He doesn't do anything except study the animals. It's shut up because he doesn't want people to get in and upset everything. That's all. That's what he told me.' The vigour of his defence of his uncle surprised Henry.

'And you believe him?' She opened her eyes, just a fraction, just so that she could look at him from between her lashes.

'Yes. Of course I do,' said Henry. It was as if he was trying to convince himself.

Behind them, the lion pawed at his eye; then, whimpering more than growling, he dragged himself over to the fence and began to rub the side of his face against the wire, rubbing and rubbing and making that noise and tearing off the scabs and bits of spoiled, matted fur. All around him the flies buzzed and darted and clung on.

'Why shouldn't I believe him?' he continued. 'I mean – is there a reason? What do they really say in the village?'

'They say that your uncle, your famous Arthur Constable, goes out into his woods at night . . . and . . .'

'And?'

'And practises black magic.'

'Oh that's ridiculous!'

'I'm only telling you what people say.'

'People say anything. They'll talk about any daft idea that comes into their heads –'

Henry stopped uncomfortably. Stella had opened her eyes and was running her fingers through her hair, not saying anything, but he knew what she was thinking: that he sounded just like his uncle.

'What I mean is, people do gossip . . .' he corrected himself.

She only fiddled with her rings, straightening them up on her little white hands.

'Everybody gossips, Stella . . . I do . . . it's probably about nothing, even if my uncle does go into the woods. Why shouldn't he? And anyway, what do you mean by "black magic"?'

'I don't mean anything. I just heard them, that's all.'

'Heard who?'

'Some people in the village. I went there with Mum a couple of weeks ago and heard people talking in a shop. And other people said the same things in school last term – not that I talk to anyone much, but they talk about me!' She got up and knocked bits angrily from her old shirt. 'Some others girls said it. They said that Mum and I must be odd because we went on living up at the park even though everyone else round here knew that your uncle practised devil worship up in the woods, at night. I told you they were all stupid cows at that school.'

Henry didn't know what to say. He'd read the sort of books that went the rounds at home. They were all about bearded men in white robes, who wore goats' heads and danced around long-haired virgins. They had seemed pretty silly after the first time, although the bits about sex had been all right. Ed was getting a taste for that sort of book now, much to their mother's horror.

But Uncle Arthur? Had he made that footprint? And in a robe? They had begun to walk back to the house and he quickened his pace. He didn't want to be late for supper, even though he wasn't at all hungry. It was a pizza and trifle evening, or was it that gâteau again? Anyway, the gossip just couldn't be true: nobody with a pair of pink oven gloves would practise black magic. Would they?

He wiped his hand across his mouth, as though his tongue was already smeared with the cloying stickiness of those sweets. He wouldn't have minded eating something else for a change, something ordinary like shepherd's pie or runner beans from the garden, with stewed apple to follow. He actually wouldn't have minded picking up windfalls and peeling them either, and abruptly, passion- ately, he wanted to leave the park. He wanted to get away; not forever, not yet, but just to get out and breathe the air on the other side of the walls. He wanted to talk to someone else. He wanted to listen to gossip in a shop. He wanted to be sure that people were as stupid as his uncle said they were.

'It's funny you should talk about Roxmere,' he

stammered, 'because I was planning to go there tomorrow. I met someone on the train – an old lady, a Mrs Ferris – and she's invited me to go and see her. Tomorrow.'

They had paused by the door to the caravan park.

'You can come too, if you like,' he said, avoiding her eyes.

'All right. What time?'

'Say two? In the afternoon – for tea – that's what Mrs Ferris said.' He wondered if she knew he was lying.

'Surely four would be a better time, if it's for tea?'

'OK. Four then.' He wasn't going to argue because it gave him more time to fix something up. She smiled and he was just going to ask her if she had actually seen his uncle going into the woods, when she slipped through the door and hurried away.

He didn't remember till half-way through supper that he had never taken the envelope with Mrs Ferris's sister's address and telephone number on it. He'd walked off like a spoilt kid, and now he'd ruined everything. Ruined, he realized now, this first chance of 'going out' with Stella. For that, surely, was what it was, even though he hadn't quite meant it like that at the time. That was definitely how he'd tell it back at school, although everything seemed so different down here. Still, at this rate, with no address, there wasn't going to be anything to tell, and he'd just revert to being what she had said he was originally: a creep. A dumb, hopeless creep.

He wasn't going to let that happen. He wanted to take Stella out more than anything in the world and would ask Julian for help. That was it. It was blindingly simple: Julian would have to help.

Henry waited until he heard his uncle go upstairs to bed at nine o'clock, then he slipped out. It was still light. Bats fluttered blackly over the terrace, and beneath the cedar the wildebeest still moved and fussed. Though the sun had set, its red glow lingered and warmed the curving grasslands and touched the pale trunks of hazel. It made the geraniums on the terrace blaze up crimson once again before night closed over the park. He tried to move quietly but his tread on the gravel wasn't silent and he glanced nervously up at the fiery windows on the first floor where he knew his uncle would be settling down to sleep.

Julian was surprised to see him.

'What's happened?' he asked quickly. 'Has something happened?'

'No. I just thought I'd . . . come and see you.'

'So this is just a social visit? And here's me thinking it's some disaster and not asking you in. Come in, come and sit down.'

The smell of paint was overwhelming. It was everywhere, in pots and palettes and tins as well as splashed over the floor and walls. It was on Julian's hands as he cleared a space for Henry, on a chair.

'Coffee? Beer?'

'Beer, please. If that's all right – I mean, if it's not, if you think – if you'd like coffee, that's fine too. Or beer.'

'Can do you?' Julian pushed some papers off a four-pack. 'Saves on the washing-up.'

It didn't look as though Julian did much washing-up.

Henry took a great gulp and somehow got the beer foaming up so that it ran down his chin and neck. He drank down through the froth to enjoy the bitterness underneath.

'Julian, can you help me?' It was not how he had intended to say it.

'That depends,' Julian looked doubtful. 'If it's to do with my father, it may be difficult.'

'It's nothing like that. It's – ' He saw her and broke off.

93

From the corner of the caravan, with that hair half covered by some sort of oriental scarf with gold in it and her white neck loaded down with necklaces, Stella gazed back at him. He took a long drink, washing away the last traces of sweetness.

'I've got to get to Roxmere,' he said. 'I've absolutely got to. In the afternoon. Tomorrow.'

Then he saw her again: now alone, now with her mother, with flowers, reading, sleeping, sprawling, standing, eating, reading again with hardly any clothes on. He broke open the second can and stared at the paintings.

'And that's why you want help, is it? To get to Roxmere?'

'Yes!' Henry wondered if he had spoken too loudly. 'Yes,' he whispered, 'yes.'

Julian smiled and stretched out his legs.

'All right, Henry. I'll take you. When?'

Henry couldn't decide, couldn't for a moment even remember why he'd come to the caravan. Julian continued to smile kindly. Now, oddly, the need to get to Roxmere seemed less urgent, and Julian was extraordinarily nice about it. Henry could not imagine why Uncle Arthur thought his son 'irresponsible' and 'difficult', even though on that first day Julian had taken him through those woods of seething, twisting snakes, where Stella had later walked almost barefooted, like she was in that picture, barefooted and barelegged and sprawling on the caravan steps.

Beer ran down on to his shirt, but he didn't mind. He almost heard the rustle of her feet as she trod into the dry leaves and on into the wet mud.

Only she hadn't. It had not been Stella's footprint in the mud. Suddenly he remembered: that was why he had to go to Roxmere – to find out.

'Shall we say two, then?'

Henry nodded.

'Or two-thirty?'

Henry nodded again, then couldn't stop, so laughed at himself for nodding so much.

'Are you all right?'

'Two or two-thirty... two to two...' The time had never struck him as ridiculous before, but now it did and he laughed at the joke of it as he tried to find the door. Julian turned him in the right direction, though he would have found it with no problem at all if only her portrait hadn't been all over the place. He couldn't put out a hand or foot without touching her. And she was beautiful. So amazingly, surprisingly beautiful. Even with that hair.

It was better outside, away from the stink of paint, and it wouldn't have been a problem to find the door in the wall either if the night hadn't been so dark. He realized that he should have accepted Julian's offer to accompany him after all, but when he turned round to accept he became so giddy that he staggered a bit and bumped into an overhanging branch of ivy. At least that meant the door in the wall couldn't be far away.

It was odd, though, that she hadn't said a word about the portraits. She had hardly mentioned Julian, yet she must have spent hours posing for him. He started to feel a way through the close, clinging ivy.

Any moment now his fingers would touch the wood of the door and he'd lift the latch and escape on to the terrace. It would be nicer on the terrace, where the sun shone; here, in the field, it was very cold.

It wasn't only his beer-soaked shirt that felt cold. There was something else in the park. Something had soaked the grass and made the ivy leaves on the wall as chill as the tongues of dead men. He drew in sharp, cold breaths of night air and struggled now to find the door as the sea mist rolled in and enclosed him. He felt its wintry touch on his burning face and, wiping it off, pushing it back, he lost contact with the wall altogether, and when he turned quickly round he lost the caravans too, and then was almost overcome by the suffocating silence.

No light shone from the house or the caravans. Now, in a gripping panic that made him gasp and sob, he wasn't even sure where the great house was.

Fear – like fear in childhood, when he'd been a really little boy and woken in the night and been too afraid, too terrified, to breathe, lest something, someone, notice the rise and fall of his chest – such a fear held him there so that like that little, helpless boy he wet himself, standing there and shivering all alone in the silent, wretched night.

And something moved, not crept or shuffled but stepped out over the gravel. Faintly at first, but louder now, something or someone who was not afraid was stepping lightly and surely over the wet gravel, and was coming, he realized, towards him.

'Please,' he sobbed, 'please no. Please don't. Please.' He put his hands out to protect himself and touched the wall. He clung on, felt the iron hinge, and realized that the door had been open all the time. At last he inhaled the sweet, night smell of honeysuckle and knew that he must have already stepped through on to the terrace.

'Please,' he begged, as though whatever it was could understand, 'please . . .'

In the mist the footsteps slowed, then stopped, and Henry knew that he was being watched.

'Please . . .' he whispered, for he was so nearly home. He moved away from the wall and heard the other turn and go back down the steps and away over the grass.

In his room he pulled off all his clothes and, shaking violently, crept between the cold sheets and curled right up with his knees almost touching his chin.

Chapter 11

The next afternoon Julian didn't appear at two or at half past, and when he still hadn't turned up at a quarter to three Henry's patience gave way.

'I bet he's forgotten,' he said. 'Did you know that he was late meeting me at the station? I had to wait for hours.'

'He'll come. Don't fuss.' Stella barely looked up from her book.

'I'm not fussing. It's just that I don't want to be late. Not for tea.'

She turned another page.

'The old lady – Mrs Ferris – will be getting tea ready for us . . .' A couple of weeks ago he wouldn't have believed that he could ever lie like this, but there was something about the park. Here, it was possible.

'It'll be three o'clock in a minute,' he groaned and thought of his father. Back there, Mr Constable always fussed about the time and worried about being late. He fussed at breakfast yet always took another piece of toast or tipped the pot right up to get a last coffee, although it had gone cold.

'Julian *will* turn up, Henry. He's probably just finishing something.' She had finally put the book aside.

Henry picked up a handful of gravel and tossed it, stone by stone, at the terrace. It all looked so different in the sun. He hit a geranium and the crimson petals splashed down on to the stones where last night some other creature had stood and watched him through the mist.

'Don't,' she said, 'you'll spoil everything.'

She wore a dress – not a dress like his mother or sisters wore, in fact, not a dress like anybody he knew had ever worn, but an odd, old-fashioned dress. It had pale, creamy lace around the neck and smelt faintly of old cupboards and lavender. It was as though she were an actress and had put on a costume for the stage. If it hadn't been for that hair, she could have been a ghost from another age: a daughter of the house from the days when Roxmere Park had been the home of a rich, country family, when there had been servants up in those attics and busy maids in the kitchens and when the children, the girls, had come running down the steps as they heard the sound of coach wheels on the drive. Those rustling, flowing skirts would have floated down behind them. In those days he was sure that the gates to the park would have stood wide open.

'See!' she cried, jumping up, 'I told you.'

The sports car drove up too quickly.

'I say!' Julian was looking at her, admiring her, openly staring at her. He nodded to Henry to climb in the back and leant over to open the door for Stella. Henry was annoyed. Actually, she had done a stupid thing, getting all dressed up like that. Henry realized with horror that everybody in the village would stare at them now. He shrank back into his corner amongst the clutter and rubbish.

'Well?' asked Julian.

'Don't ask me,' Stella laughed, 'It's Henry's great idea!'

'It isn't my great idea at all! It's only tea.' Sometimes, often, he really hated her.

'Sure it's tea, but where?' Julian asked patiently. 'What's the address?'

Henry had rehearsed this bit and so went through the

99

pretence of looking in all his pockets for the envelope which he knew was not there. They waited with the engine running and both watched him.

'Perhaps it's in your room?' suggested Stella.

'It isn't. I know it isn't.'

Stella and Julian looked away.

'OK then.' Julian swung the car swiftly round towards the gates and the wind blew the lace up around her white neck and she smiled at him and joked and talked to him as easily as with an old friend.

Henry, cramped in the back, held his arm up against the sun overhead that was too hot and burnt his face and made his heart pound wildly. This time they did not turn off into the track through the woods, but drove towards the main gates. As they approached them Henry's anxiety increased. He was painfully and miserably afraid that they would not be able to get out of the park. He almost expected someone to rush out, shouting and barring their way, but no one did. The gates opened and closed and Julian turned on to the main road.

It was cooler outside and Henry immediately felt better. A breeze carried the freshness of the sea and Julian drove more slowly and teased Stella about wearing great black walking boots under such a pretty dress. He caught Henry's eye in the mirror and asked again about the address, and Henry took a deep breath of the clearer air and confessed that actually, he hadn't got an address and that the only information he had was the old lady's name, Mrs Ferris.

They didn't ridicule him or call him an idiot although he suspected that he deserved it. He was certain that they had sensed he was lying all along, yet they didn't question him at all. They drove in silence now, following the long dip of the road down into Roxmere.

Julian parked outside a newsagent's in the High Street and went in to make inquiries. Stella silently twisted her rings.

Then Henry looked up and saw them. He saw Mrs Ferris and her sister on the other side of the street, in one of those strange coincidences that don't surprise as much as they might. He leapt from the car and ran across, calling her name loudly, so that the two old ladies looked around in bewilderment.

'It's *me*, Mrs Ferris!'

But she didn't recognize him and stepped back.

'You gave me your address . . . I mean . . .' If only she had.

'Isn't it that boy from the train?' prompted her sister. 'The one who was going up to the park?' They both examined him: two shrewd old women with pale, yellowed eyes.

'Why, of course it is. It's Henry, isn't it?' She smiled then and took his hand and looked up into his face.

'What's happened, dear? Is everything all right?'

'Oh yes. It's wonderful up there. It's just . . .'

'Yes dear?'

'I wondered . . . well, you did say that if I was ever, you know, at a loose end, one afternoon . . .'

People jostled them on the hot pavement and she followed his glance as he looked back quickly at Stella. Then she straightened the brim of her shabby hat and exchanged a look with her sister and said, 'Maybe you'd like to come to tea? . . . If you're at a loose end? With your friend?'

'Oh thank you, Mrs Ferris. Thank you very much. In, say, half an hour?' And he would have dashed straight off again had she not smiled, then laughed knowingly up at him. He shrugged and laughed back.

Suddenly he didn't mind at all, and when she took the

original envelope from the pocket of her frayed old coat he realized that she wasn't the least bit horrible or mad. Her sister pointed to the row of slate-roofed cottages further down the road and he could have flung his arms about her and whirled her round like people in films do to little old ladies.

Julian looked relieved that Henry had, as he said, 'got things sorted', and he drove off leaving the two of them with half an hour to kill. It was crowded in Roxmere: July, Stella explained, was the beginning of the tourist season, and several times they were edged off the pavement by families loaded up with all the bright, plastic burdens of chairs and toys and picnics that they took with them to the beach. Small children licked and dropped ice-creams and older ones spun the merry-go-rounds of postcards that stood outside the shops. It smelt of coconut sun-oil and vinegar and, now and then, the sea.

People did look at Stella. Middle-aged women with shiny, pink knees and men with even fatter, pinker stomachs turned to look, scowling and nudging each other. Henry recognized their disapproval: that was how people always looked at Ali Draper. They inspected her and then turned away with a sneer and he remembered, with shame, that he had done that too, and he quickened his step to keep up with Stella. She always walked so quickly with her head held straight up.

The tea was wonderful. It was set out on a table with an embroidered cloth and gold-edged china, just as though they had really been expected. There was bread and butter cut very thinly and little pots of fish paste and jam, then chocolate biscuits and shortbread, and finally home-made sponge cake with a large wedge already eaten and jam seeping out between the tiers. Henry ate as if he had been starved, and though he knew it must look very rude, he couldn't stop, and took yet another slice and let them pour him just one more cup of tea.

He didn't say much but it didn't matter because Stella was more talkative than he'd ever seen her. She had grown up, it turned out, in parts of London that Mrs Ferris and her sister knew well, and they gossiped about places that he had never heard of, joking about things he barely understood. He just ate himself silly, wondering with rising panic how he could ever ask about the gossip concerning the park.

In the end he didn't have to. Mrs Ferris's brother-in-law came in from his allotment smelling strongly of beer and mud, and as he washed noisily in the sink in the kitchen he called out cheerfully:

'And what's that mad uncle of yours up to nowadays, young man?'

The two ladies tut-tutted but he strode in, rubbing a towel over his red face and neck, and repeated the question. Stella looked up at him and said sweetly:

'Well actually, he's given up child sacrifice and he's drinking monkey blood instead to keep him young!'

They all laughed, especially the old man, who asked Stella if she couldn't get him a little bottle of it, just for a Saturday night. Mrs Ferris and her sister shrieked with laughter, then, remembering that he was Arthur Constable's nephew, they glanced at Henry in embarrassment, and said that, of course, it was only idle country gossip.

'Is it?' he asked, and that moment of quiet deepened into a silence that spread over the table.

'Is it?' he asked again. 'Is it just gossip, about him doing those things up there in the woods?'

'Yes, of course it is, dear,' said Mrs Ferris carefully. 'People will say anything.'

103

She got up and began to put the plates together and Henry knew that his chance was slipping away.

'What *do* they say?'

'They gossip.'

'But what do they actually say? Please.' He looked at each of them and then Mrs Ferris sat down again, still holding on to the pile of plates.

'People do say, Henry, that your uncle does strange things up there in the park—'

'It used not be like that,' interrupted her sister. 'The park used to be really nice when it first opened, with all those animals. Lots of people from the village worked there then and got good money. In those days the village was just a stream of cars going up there. They used to queue all the way up the hill, on a hot day, and break down too – '

'So what happened?'

'Well, he closed the park, didn't he?'

'But why?'

'Nobody knows that, not down here they don't. Only, it was after he closed it that the trouble began . . .'

'What trouble? What happened?'

'Well, nothing actually *happened* – not that we know of – only people began to say that they'd seen your uncle up in the wood with –' She looked nervously at Mrs Ferris. 'With ghosts, people said . . .'

'Ghosts?'

'That's what people said – not that I believe them, but all the same. No smoke without fire.'

'After all,' added her husband, 'he had been to all those foreign places. Places where they do things differently – not that I'm criticizing. And he'd brought back strange things, hadn't he, statues and heads and what have you. They used to be on show sometimes, though people round here didn't think much of them. Ugly, they were, just plain ugly. And people said that over there, in those foreign places, he'd learnt black magic – or voodoo – or whatever you call it. They said that he'd come home and started practising it in the woods. People saw him.'

'Who saw him?' asked Mrs Ferris.

'I can't quite remember. Not now. It was some time ago. But it definitely happened. Everybody said so.' The old man was a little defensive.

'That's right,' said his wife. 'It was before all those new fences were put up, when you could still get into the park. Lads from the village used to climb in at night for a lark. I don't need to tell you what boys'll do for a thrill, now do I?' She smiled at Henry.

'Nowadays,' continued Mrs Ferris's sister, 'everybody is too scared. Nobody from the village will go up there.'

'Except me,' said Stella.

'And you've never seen anything?' They all looked at her expectantly.

'No,' she murmured. 'No I haven't. Not like that – '

'Well, I don't believe any of it!' interrupted Henry. He spoke loudly, trying to silence his own doubts, and Stella looked away and bit into her nails.

At the door, as they said goodbye, Mrs Ferris put the envelope firmly into his hand and reminded him that he was welcome to come again, at any time.

'Although,' she laughed, nodding at Stella, 'it looks as though you've found someone even prettier to buy coffee for.'

For a moment he was horrified, then he saw Stella smile. He saw her toss back her brilliant hair and bite down the smile on her lips and he knew that she was quite extraordinarily beautiful. He grinned boldly back at Mrs Ferris in a way that was not like him and joked in some other person's voice, that the first coffee was always the sweetest. Mrs Ferris chuckled and patted his arm and told him to be off, and he ran after Stella and wished that the whole world would look round and stare at him as he walked beside this girl in her floating dress.

It was a very long walk back. He had been so anxious to get away from the park and find Mrs Ferris that he had never thought about getting back to it and now, after an hour's walk, he was sorry. Stella didn't mind. She said that she often walked back from school if she missed the bus. She rolled up the sleeves of her dress and laughed about having worn the right boots after all. Then, he didn't mind either. He could have walked by her side for ever, could have walked with her to the end of the road and on over the sea and never looked back, had he not become aware of some sound from behind the walls of the park. Somebody was working there, in the woods, just over the brow of the hill.

Something was moving in there. Stella heard it too and fell quiet, and instantly all Henry's joy was stamped out as though a mountain of mud had slithered down and blocked the clear bright road ahead so that he must turn aside and fight his way through the entangled branches and shifting, treacherous layers of leaves.

Then they heard it again: the ring of metal or stone on wood, surely that was it. Stella put her hand on his arm and kept close beside him.

It could have been anything: maybe Arthur Constable was strengthening the fences, or maybe it was the animals after all. The chimpanzees could be displaying. His uncle had warned him that the males sometimes rushed about, beating and banging things in order to gain control over the rest of the troupe.

They saw the wheel marks first, then that the unofficial way into the park was unlocked. The buttercup and willow-herb on the verge had only recently been flattened down. Their leaves had scarcely begun to wither; some, indeed, were already springing back, covering up the two lines that led from the road to the narrow wooden gate that now stood ajar. It must have been Julian. After leaving them in Roxmere he must have driven back in a hurry, taken this short cut, and then not bothered to secure the gate. Or had he too been distracted? Had he too heard something unusual when he got out of the car? Had he gone to investigate and left the way free?

Still, it wasn't anything to do with them. All Henry had to do was shut the gate securely – lock it maybe, if the key was there. Then they could continue down the road to the main gate. It wasn't that much further. And it really wasn't Henry's problem if Julian defied his father and went through the woods – except that beyond them the woods lay in wait.

Henry's teeth were chattering as he stepped round the edge of the door. She followed, gathering up her skirt so that it did not catch. They moved as silently as moths at dusk, Henry with his arm up before his face in case something should leap out at them. The sound continued its rhythmic repetition, drawing them on. It couldn't, he was sure, be the chimpanzees. They couldn't produce so regular a note and for so long. The tone reminded him more of a woodpecker or, he realized with horror, a rattlesnake, though that was absurd. It was totally impossible in these leafy English woods where bluebells grew in spring. Stella had told him that around Easter it was so blue that it looked as though patches of sky had fallen down. He wouldn't have minded staying on and seeing it, actually.

'Henry!' She was shaking his arm, dragging him back.

When he looked up he saw a small clearing around a tree that had recently been felled. The curls of peeled-back bark lay bright and white on the fallen leaves. The man who was working there looked up at them, nodded and said something, then resumed his work. One black hand repositioned the chisel edge on the raw wood and the other brought the mallet down in a sweep of swift, sure blows. The outline of a second eye was scored more deeply into the wood. The man glanced at them again and Henry thought that he was about to approach them, but he didn't. He only pushed back the torn sleeve of his old shirt and then moved to the other side of the carving and ran his fingers gently over the high, domed skull. The blows echoed again but his bare feet scarcely disturbed the dry leaves.

They watched him from a distance, not daring to step closer, and he continued to work the figure out of the wood, wholly absorbed in the task. In the end he turned his back on them, as though they were of little importance, and they made their way out towards the sunshine.

Chapter 12

'It's like Robinson Crusoe,' Stella said at last. They had walked back in silence and now lingered at the door to the caravan park.

'Robinson who?'

'Robinson Crusoe. You must have read about him and Man Friday, on that desert island.'

Henry nodded, remembering now.

'And do you remember when Crusoe saw that footprint in the sand?' she whispered.

'Like we did, in the mud?'

She frowned unhappily and looked at him. Henry caught his breath and could hardly speak.

'That man's not some tramp passing through, is he?' he murmured eventually.

She shrugged and looked away, twisting her rings.

'He's living here, isn't he? He's been living in those woods for ages. Hasn't he?'

She looked up at him and there were tears in her eyes, and she nodded. They had both seen the evidence: a sort of shack on the edge of the clearing, and the way he had behaved. He had been at home, almost, in that wood.

'And you *knew*.' Henry's diffidence was turning to anger.

'No!'

'You did. You knew all the time.'

She shook her head but he kept on angrily.

'You've known for ages. You must have done. You

couldn't have been here for a year and not have known. But who is he? What's he doing there?'

'I didn't know,' she protested, but he wouldn't listen.

'That's why you weren't afraid to go in the woods. You knew that there weren't any snakes in there. My uncle was just making that up to scare me away, to keep me out of the woods so that I wouldn't discover him. But you knew. Everybody must have known. Except me.' He was wild with the hurt of having been tricked.

'I really didn't know, Henry.'

'You must have done, the whole lot of you knew: my uncle, Julian, you – everyone knew! You must all think I'm so stupid. And I bet that's why my uncle invited me, because I'm the stupid one in the Constable family. And that's why my parents let me come. I bet they knew too and they thought, "Oh, Henry's dumb. He'll never notice that there's some strange black man, some savage, living secretly in the woods." That's why the park is all shut up, isn't it? So that man can't escape and run wild. It's a prison, isn't it? With him kept in here! And you knew!'

He caught hold of her and tried to drag her round to face him, but she jerked violently away and he saw with horror that he'd made a red mark on her white arm.

'I didn't know,' she shouted back. 'And I still don't know what that poor man is doing in the woods. I've had this feeling that something in the park wasn't right, but I didn't know *what*, not for sure.' She moved away from him, towards the door. 'But I know something else, Henry Constable, and it's that you *are* a creep, after all. You're as horrid as your horrid uncle and every day that passes you get more horrid. You're getting just like *him*. You should hear yourself, you pompous prat, talking about "savages" and "black men running wild". It's disgusting and so are

110

you. You and your whole rotten family stink! It's people like you who spoil everything.' She turned from him but he followed her.

'You don't even know my family. My family doesn't spoil anything: they're good at things. My family . . .' His voice trailed away. His family, he realized, were far away. They were too far away and so safe and sound and they'd let him come down here, to all this. They hadn't cared about what might happen to him.

'I do know you and your uncle and they're family,' she persisted.

'And Julian? You know him, don't you?' he said nastily. He hated her so much.

'What about Julian?' She looked surprised.

'Everyone knows that artists are rotten people,' he continued. 'Why don't you mention him? Or is he your boyfriend or something?' He couldn't stop himself and just blundered on. 'How could you let him paint those pictures of you? It's disgusting! I guessed you were like that as soon as I saw you – and saw your hair. Though I suppose Julian thinks it's wonderful and "artistic" like he thought this stupid dress was wonderful. Nobody wears dresses like this.'

He had tugged at a bit of the dress and was about to pull up the hem, like some horrid little boy in primary school, when he heard someone laughing behind him.

'Now now, Henry!' It was his uncle. Arthur Constable had walked up behind them without being noticed and now he was chuckling merrily.

'What's all this about? Or need I ask?' He grinned and Henry felt a bright stain of embarrassment flood over his face as he dropped the handful of dress. 'I can see that my nephew still needs educating in the matter of young ladies,' he joked. He put one hand on Henry's shoulder and would have put the other on Stella had she not stepped quickly out of his reach. Arthur Constable only grinned more widely.

'I hope he hasn't been pestering you, Stella?'

Henry saw her draw breath to reply. He saw the contempt in her eyes and knew that it was not just for his uncle. There was some for him too and he deserved it. He waited, hopelessly, with that old hand like a brand on his shoulder, but she didn't speak. She pressed her lips together and swallowed the reply, and at that moment Mrs Elder interrupted them. She came to the caravan door, looked out anxiously and beckoned her daughter in. Stella went at once, but looked back at Henry.

'*I* wear dresses like this,' she hissed, 'because *I* like them! And I'm not afraid of what anybody thinks!'

'Women,' groaned Arthur Constable, in mock horror. 'Don't they always try to have the last word!'

'She isn't like that,' said Henry.

'It's all right, old man. You don't have to pretend to me. They're *all* "like that". Women, girls: they're not like us. In the end, all they care about is dresses.'

'She meant something else,' muttered Henry, miserably. He knew his uncle wasn't listening to him.

'They can cause trouble, too,' continued his uncle. 'They don't mean to, so don't get me wrong. I'm not against women, it's just that you have to recognize them for what they are. You'll agree with me, Henry, when you're older. When you have a little bit more experience, you'll see that I'm right. That girl doesn't care about anything important. She isn't capable of it!'

Arthur Constable smiled again as people smile into mirrors, with their mouths curved and their eyes unmoved. He kept his hand on his great-nephew's shoulder so that when he turned to go back to the house, the boy had to turn too. Henry fretted to throw off that constraint like a horse frets at a tightened rein, yet he dared not.

'She does care,' he mouthed silently, hating himself for his cowardice.

He was sure that anybody else would have tackled his uncle. Tom or Adam would have. Even the unbearable, unstoppable Ed would have had more guts. 'Hey,' he'd have cried, 'who's that man living in a shack in the woods?' And Ed wouldn't have been fobbed off and side-tracked. He'd have kept on and on until he got an answer. Ed was as persistent as toothache.

'Well, Henry?' His uncle tightened his grip, not intending to hurt him, surely, but pinching the skin against his collar bone in a way that was not pleasant.

Henry jerked away and rubbed the place.

'Well?' repeated his uncle. 'Don't you agree with me?'

He only had to say 'no' to stand up to the old man. He drew a breath.

'Not really. Not . . .' His heart beat so fast that he couldn't continue, and he stepped further back just in case.

'Not yet?' suggested his uncle, magnanimously. 'Don't worry about it, Henry. You *will* do. And don't feel ashamed. I like a person who has their own opinions. In time, I know you'll come to agree with me. You just haven't had enough experience of life yet and that's not your fault. But you *will* agree with me. Later. There's no other way of looking at things. Years and years of study and observation have brought me to conclude that it's natural, Henry, natural, for some forms of life to be more highly developed. Shakespeare and Darwin weren't women, were they? More's the pity, but that's a fact, and fridges weren't invented in Africa.' He grinned. 'Nor,' he added, 'do leopards change their spots. Ever.'

It felt to Henry like being swept away by the remorseless waters of a deepening flood. He might scream and manage a few strokes towards the bank. He might even cling to a piece of driftwood, but in the end he would be overwhelmed. It hardly mattered what he said or did because Arthur Constable would be unaffected by it. The old man had defended himself from differing opinions by erecting a wall of such solidity that he could no longer hear or feel what other people might think. It made Henry despair.

During supper, while his uncle went on and on about his theory of the different and fixed places of men and women and animals in the world, Henry was doubled up by a violent wave of nausea. For the last couple of days he had been finding it harder and harder to finish those meals which he had so enjoyed at first. Now something slimy and half-cooked had smeared itself over his tongue and down his throat. Then it had stuck. He clamped his hand to his mouth and jumped up.

'What people refuse to accept,' continued his uncle, not taking any notice, 'is that the places of people are just as fixed as those of plants and animals. Nobody expects oranges to grow at the North Pole, but they expect people to adapt. Scientists wouldn't try to genetically engineer a meat-eating mouse because that would be a monster. But they do it with people, Henry, they really do. They give primitive people a taste for education and wealth and then there's no stopping them. It's a tragedy, Henry. Henry?'

Henry had already fled from the kitchen. He ran along the dark corridor, out of the empty, echoing hall into the mild evening. He clung to the terrace wall and retched drily as though his insides were being torn out, strand by strand: maybe he was going to die agonizingly of food poisoning. His mother had always warned against the dangers of fast food. He rested his sweaty forehead on the warm stone and felt iller than he'd ever felt before.

Then he heard his uncle.

'Henry? Henry?' The sharp voice echoed in the hall. The determined tread ground into the gravel.

Instinctively, like an animal seeking cover, Henry dropped down to the far side of the wall and crouched there, out of sight.

'Henry?'

He heard his uncle walk to and fro and call again, more irritably, and then curse unpleasantly and go in.

An evening breeze moved lazily through the unfurled honeysuckle and beneath it, bathed in its scent, Henry crawled away on all fours, as stealthy and cautious as a feral cat.

Stella had been right. He spat awkwardly and wiped his mouth with the back of his hand. 'Horrid' and 'disgusting' were the words she had used. He arched his back where his shirt stuck, clammy with sweat. He could smell himself and was disgusted too. Once safely through the door into the caravan park he straightened up and was finally, violently sick. Like some little kid who had stuffed himself silly, he vomited again and again.

Mrs Elder rescued him. She took him by the arm and sat him down on the caravan steps and brought out warm water, soap and a clean T-shirt. She clearly didn't think he was dying, and now neither did he. In fact, with that sour taste gone, he was actually hungry. Inside they were eating. He could hear the chink of knives and forks on plates, but they didn't invite him in. He was disappointed and on the point of leaving when Stella came out.

She'd been crying. He saw it at once: her eyes had gone small and her white skin was all blotchy.

'Mum wants to know if you wanted some proper supper,' she said, not looking at him, twisting her rings.

He did. He was starving, as though he hadn't been fed in days, and he knew what he wanted.

'Could I have bacon? Fried bacon?'

'Bacon?' she scowled.

'Like you had that other morning – last week. You had fried bacon for breakfast, didn't you?'

'Yes. How did you know?'

'I smelt it that first morning I was here. I thought it was for me, and I was really happy.'

'You were in for a shock then,' she remarked with satisfaction, and seeing her smile he said quickly, 'I didn't mean it about the dress. Or about – '

'Mum,' Stella called, stopping him. 'Mum, he wants bacon, of all things. Fried bacon!'

'Then he can cook it himself,' Mrs Elder retorted, but when they went in she was already melting the fat in the pan.

'We ought to go back there,' said Stella quietly, cutting bread for him.

He nodded. It was what he wanted to do – what he had to do: to go back and find out everything, if that were possible.

They waited until the lights went off in the big house, so by the time they had reached the edge of the wood it was already dark. It seemed impossible that they should find a way through, let alone catch another glimpse of the man, but they had to try. Henry had never liked the dark and now he moved in fits and starts, ducking clumsily under low branches and stumbling over roots and into rabbit holes. His face and hands were scratched and bruised and he realized that although it was hard to go into the wood, it would be even harder to find a way out.

'Good thing I haven't still got the dress on,' Stella whispered. He understood, then, that he was forgiven. He reached out in the dark and found her hand, and she held on tightly as though she was as apprehensive as he.

Henry was the first to smell the smoke. It reminded him of autumn afternoons back home when they had burnt the leaves and stood as close as they dared to the darting bonfire flames. He remembered the way the smoke always billowed to and fro and how his mother would worry about upsetting the neighbours and how his father always wanted to take charge of the fire and prevent them throwing fresh green stuff on. Now, in the dark, they couldn't see any smoke, though the smell of burning was pungent. Then they saw embers. On the edge of what appeared to be the same clearing, the remains of a small fire glowed and flickered redder than any snake's eye.

Henry looked intently into the darkness, and was certain that the man was somewhere near. Stella had stepped close so that the spiky tips of her hair touched his cheek, and he felt her breath come and go rapidly. He knew that she too was watching, forcing herself to see.

Moving very slowly, at first unsure and blind, and starting away from every shifting leaf and black, cracked twig, they were slowly becoming accustomed to the darkness of the wood. They passed on from scared imaginings to discerning and then distinguishing the shapes within, and they were the shapes of another world. When a gust of wind ran through the undergrowth, a spark flared up and a flame caught and climbed, and in its light, finally, they saw the outline of the man. He was standing there quietly, watching them. He was a slight man of medium height and now it seemed to Henry that he had seen him before: that he

117

almost knew him. Then, as he stepped towards them and drew the blanket, or whatever it was, around his shoulders, Henry recognized the figure he had seen on the night of the storm. This was the man who had walked over the grass towards the cedar tree – and who had raised his arms up to the rain as it poured down on him.

He said something to them that they couldn't understand, and threw more wood on the fire so that it blazed up again. Then he beckoned them over to him. The sign was unmistakable. They went right up to the flames so that he might examine them more closely. It was Stella whom he really looked at. He held up a branch from the fire and in its brief light reached out with his other hand and touched her hair. He smiled fleetingly, but not at either of them – he smiled at some memory recalled from too far away, as though he saw more than their faces in the firelight.

Stella didn't flinch or step back, but stood there determinedly, twisting her rings and returning the man's regard. He was at least middle-aged, with a deeply lined face and white curls in his beard and hair. The palm of his right hand, which he eventually extended to Henry, was heavily calloused: a craftsman's hand with a firm grip. He spoke to them, greeting them maybe, and then repeated the same words, though Henry did not understand what he said. Behind the man Henry glimpsed more carvings standing against the side of the shack, and though he pointed to them and smiled, hoping that they might have provided another means of communication, the man ignored his attempt. He did not open the door of the shack for them, nor pile more wood on the fire and suggest that they sit down by it or even draw near. Yet he had been sitting there; as Henry's eyes became more accustomed to the flickering light he saw a plate and mug set on a slab of wood that clearly was used as a table. This man had been sitting out here eating on this fine summer evening and they were certainly not being invited to the feast. Indeed, there was something about the way that he stood there which implied that they were not so welcome.

Stella understood it first. 'Come on. I think we ought to go.' She had already turned away.

'But we can't just leave him . . .' Henry was outraged. It was all wrong. This prisoner, this abandoned and lost man, should at least have been begging them to stay.

Instead he was leading them out of the wood. He moved with silent ease, waiting for them every now and then and pointing out hidden ditches or clumps of brambles which would have hurt them. On the edge of the wood he stopped and from the protection of the trees pointed out the way back. When they looked around to thank him they could not see him.

'Has he gone, do you think?' asked Stella.

They sensed rather than saw the outline of the house in the distance. Suddenly it felt dangerously exposed to be out in this open blackness of the meadows at night. They looked around for him again, but there was nothing.

'Has he really gone?' whispered Stella, finding his hand in the dark.

'No. I think he's just there, watching us!' Henry put his arm around her shoulder.

Behind them the woods shifted in unsteady sleep and yet further away still the waves were drawn on to break unseen against the shore. A black breeze touched Henry's face and he brushed it off and touched the softness of her hair.

'You didn't know, did you, Stella?'

He felt her shake her head sadly.

'But I guessed,' she said, turning towards him.

'How?'

'From Julian's pictures, I suppose.'

'What pictures?'

'He painted a series of pictures of an African family – at least that's what I always thought it was. I never asked and he never said. I just sort of imagined that he'd painted them when he was in Africa with his father.'

'And?'

'And then one day last spring when I was sitting for him I noticed this really odd thing: he'd painted these figures *here*.'

'How do you mean, "here"?'

'They were in this park. You know where the River Rox goes into the sea, where you mustn't swim because of the currents?'

'No!'

'Hasn't your uncle warned you about it?'

'No. Not a word.'

'Oh. Oh well, I'll show you, if you like, because it's really beautiful. Only you can't swim there. Anyway – he'd painted these figures there. I mean, anyone could recognize it from the cliffs and the shingle. When I asked him about it he got really annoyed and that's not like him at all. It was obvious that he didn't want to talk about it, and the next time I went to sit for him the pictures weren't there. But I've wondered about them ever since. Mum has too. She's even seen your uncle going down to the woods at night – all that business of going to bed at nine o'clock is a sham, you know. He gets up again. Mum says he goes out later. But we couldn't ask.'

'Why not?'

They were near the house now, near enough to smell the wildebeest under the cedar and near enough to see a window on the front of the house slowly open. The moon had come up and now caught the movement of the glass as someone slid up the heavy frame.

And why not? It was a hot, close night; anyone could reasonably want more air. Yet they held their breath as they passed the cedar and approached the edge of the steps. They had disturbed the animals, who moved and stamped. From somewhere or nowhere an unexpected breeze strengthened and passed them and suddenly the curtain billowed out of the opened window. Only then did Henry realize that it was his window. Somebody was up there in his room looking out: looking out, in all probability, for him.

'It must be my uncle.' That was not unreasonable either. He had run out of the house and not returned when his uncle had called him. The old man would naturally have been concerned, wouldn't he?

He knew that he ought to go in at once and face him, yet he didn't. He couldn't. He was afraid to step across the gravel and draw the attention of whoever watched at that window.

'I must go back, Henry.' Stella gently withdrew her arm.

'No, don't go.'

'I must. Mum will worry.'

'Please Stella, not yet.' Unexpectedly, painfully, he envied her. Back home his own mother would have worried.

'About those pictures, Stella, Julian's pictures, why couldn't you ask him?'

'And risk Mum losing her job?'

'But . . .' He did not understand.

'Look. We can talk about it tomorrow. I have to go now. And we can go back to the woods. It'll be easier in daylight.'

'Stella, please!' But it was no good. Her little, ringed

fingers slipped from his grasp and she ran off over the gravel, not caring who heard.

Henry slumped down behind the wall. In a moment she'd be running up the caravan steps. Back home they'd be going to bed too: there would be the usual chaos of people hammering on the bathroom door. His father would be telling Tom to 'turn the volume down, for heaven's sake' and Ed would be reading comics in the toilet. Rose might still be practising her scales in the lounge. When he was little it had been like listening to a lullaby, listening to her scales rising and falling, rising and falling.

He rested his head against the brickwork. He could smell the cushions of moss and the things that had stuck and dried in the cracks. He yawned and yawned again and pressing his hand over his mouth tasted the mud from the woods, but couldn't be bothered, not any more, and settled down so that the side of his face that was scratched was not rubbed too much by the sharp edges. Once he thought he heard the window sliding shut, but then again, it could have been something else.

Chapter 13

Henry awoke from a nightmare of drowning by eventually finding, just when his strength had almost gone, a crack in the rocks. He crammed his fingers in and hung on, against the drag of the freezing current. When he opened his eyes and saw that the sun was up, he shivered. He had never ever felt so cold. He was almost too stiff to move. His forehead and elbows hurt and it took him a moment to realize that it was the gravel at the base of the wall, and not shingle from the beach, that was pressing into his skin.

He stretched cautiously: his neck felt broken or, at least, not right. At home his mother would have been concerned. At home this would never have happened. Then he saw the chimpanzees. They stood in a group a few yards off and watched him with curiosity. Mild apprehension made a couple of them raise their arms threateningly and draw back their lips to expose their teeth. They had been moving towards the house and needed to pass him. He glanced at his watch. Any minute now Uncle Arthur would be coming out to feed them. He did not want to be discovered sleeping out like some tramp.

Then he remembered. Somewhere down in the woods, that man would be waking too. He hunched himself up with his knees under his chin and looked down, and the chimpanzees edged past and up on to the terrace. His uncle would be out with their fruit in a moment. Usually it was bananas. Twice a week the old man drove off to get these and other supplies. He worked hard to preserve this paradise behind the wall. There was the sound of the door and that was his step upon the gravel. He'd feed them and gently, lovingly spend time with his favourites, who sometimes nuzzled up against him, touching him with their clever, knowing hands. He was so good to them. And was he good to the man in the wood? Did he also go down there with food in his arms?

And why had nobody done anything? Why had nobody taken that man by the hand and led him to freedom? He must be there against his will, so he must want to escape. Was he a prisoner or the subject of some bizarre scientific experiment? Had he been a servant or, more likely, a slave, brought back by his uncle? People must have seen him, for after all he and Stella had discovered the man without that much difficulty. Or had people known and just not cared? Had they preferred to talk about black magic and devils in the woods? Was that easier than knowing?

He wished he hadn't found out. He wished that he had heeded the warnings about the snakes and not gone into the woods with Stella. If he hadn't found out he could have just drifted through this summer. He could have dozed away the warm afternoons and enjoyed all those junk meals, even if they did make him throw up now and again; he could have gone down to Roxmere with the proper tourists and eaten chips and found himself a tiny space on the beach and stripped off. He could have burnt himself stupid, without his parents stopping him, sunbathed with Stella beside him maybe, which would have been really something, if he hadn't known the truth.

Only he did. He knew and it was all spoiled now, spoiled like everything he had ever tried to do.

'Henry?'

'Oh! Uncle Arthur! I . . .'

'No need to jump like that, Henry. You'll frighten the chimps.' His uncle smiled expansively. 'Lovely morning. Got any plans?' His uncle seemed in a particularly good mood. He couldn't have forgotten about last night, so maybe he didn't mind. Now seemed the best moment to ask about the man in the wood.

'Uncle Arthur?'

'No, Henry. No apologies.'

'But I – '

'No, my lad, I won't listen to any apologies. I was just like you at this age.' He came close and put a comforting, supporting arm around Henry's shoulders. 'I knew you'd follow in my footsteps. As soon as I saw you I said, "That's the lad for me". And wasn't I right? Here you are, doing exactly what I did: I also used to creep out of the house early to observe the animals. It's in the blood, Henry. Scientific observation is in the blood!'

'But Uncle – ' He felt desperate. It was like drowning in air while the sun rose hotter and hotter.

'No, Henry. No "buts".' His uncle patted his shoulder and adjusted his spectacles. 'I've made up my mind – though my solicitor thinks I'm a rash man. But never mind these local chaps, that's what I always say, Henry. Do what your heart tells you. And my heart told me that you were the Constable for me.' He stepped back and pointed to the great house and then to the beautiful park. 'One day, Henry, one day, because even I can't go on for ever, one day, Henry Constable, all this could be yours!'

It was so awful that he didn't laugh, although he thought he was going to. Visions of Adam and Ed and Tom, and of how they would have hooted with laughter, only made it worse. But they soon faded and he smiled back, feebly. His uncle was not put off.

'At one time, Henry, I had hopes of my son Julian, but I've been disappointed, bitterly disappointed: betrayed by him, people might say – though I don't. Not really betrayed, but we won't go into that. It's you, Henry, and your future that we need to talk about.'

'My future?'

'Why yes. Your future lies here, Henry. As the next owner of Roxmere Park. But I have to be sure that everything would be safe in your hands.'

'My hands?'

'Of course. Are your hands safe, Henry?'

'No!'

'Rubbish. Absolute stuff and nonsense. Your trouble, Henry, is lack of confidence. You don't know what you can do, but I know. So you'll just have to trust me. Now, let me see, I'll meet you by the jeep in thirty-five minutes, as usual, shall I?'

Henry shook his head in horrified disbelief.

'All right, forty minutes. I don't mind.' His uncle hurried off with the jaunty step of someone who has finally managed to settle some problems.

Henry went into the kitchen to find something to eat. Mrs Elder had left his breakfast tray on the table as usual. Once, years ago, when he was really young, somebody at home had dropped a jar of marmalade on the kitchen floor and left it there, splash, right in the middle. Henry had run past and got it on his shoes and been blamed. He could remember the sensation now: stickiness on the soles so that every time he shifted from foot to foot, something still stuck. He had protested in vain and he still remembered the unspeakable, shameful fury he had felt at not being believed. Later there had been the humiliation of being forgiven for something he had not done. Worst of all, perhaps, had been his growing fear that he might actually have taken and dropped the jar and forgotten. Everybody else had been so certain, and he so helpless.

It wasn't so different now. Despair crouched behind him, pushing his stiff neck down, so that it ached even more. He had failed totally. He hadn't asked what he needed to ask. He hadn't even made his uncle listen to him. He might as well have hurled himself at the cedar and tried to tear it down with his bare hands.

And he might as well go home now: just give up and go. He'd got a return ticket. At home he'd own up that it hadn't been much of a visit, that they had been right, after all. Roxmere Park wasn't a suitable place. They'd be pleased. They'd work hard at making it up to him. Soon he could forget all about it, if he tried. Anyway, he'd be so tired when he got home, after last night and the journey, he'd need a good sleep. He'd probably need a whole day in bed, then he'd just do the normal holiday things, watch telly, go swimming, see Adam, talk about girls. He could tell Adam about Stella and –

And never see her again? Not just not go swimming with her, but never again stand so close that his cheek would be touched by the cockatoo's plumage of colour that sprang from her head. It would be like she was dead, or he was. That was what people in films said about breaking up: that they couldn't go on living, though of course they did. The odd thing about people at school was that as soon as they broke up with a girl they said that really she was a slag and a bitch and they couldn't think why they'd taken her out in the first place. He'd never say that about Stella; he couldn't – and couldn't leave, either. He wouldn't climb down again, not with her watching.

He joined his uncle for the tour of inspection as arranged. It went off as pleasantly as always. Strangely, Arthur Constable made no further reference to the future of Roxmere Park, and Henry was relieved. More peculiar, though, was his uncle's insistence that Henry had left the house early when they both knew this to be untrue. Henry was pleased that the apparent disappearance of several goats caused a slight diversion.

'Probably just wandered off,' said the old man, scrambling back down a steep bank where he had been looking for them. He was agile and fit. Nobody would have guessed that he was over seventy.

'I'll look for them after lunch,' offered Henry, sensing an opportunity.

'Good man. Only don't fall down the cliffs.'

'I wouldn't go to the cliffs. I'd search the woods.' He looked closely at his uncle as he spoke.

'And why,' asked the old man, drumming his finger and thumb vigorously on the steering wheel, 'would you do that?'

'I thought I heard something unusual in there the other day.'

'Then you thought wrong.' His uncle turned the wheel sharply. 'These are mountain goats. They don't like woods. They get caught up in the undergrowth. I've seen a goat starve to death because it got caught in blackberries. It was only young: the more it struggled to escape, the deeper the barbs went in. Of course goats are stupid, really. You only have to look at the size of their brains.'

'So they do go into the woods, sometimes.' Henry tried to keep his voice steady.

Arthur Constable didn't reply at once. Then, as they approached the house, he slowed right down and turned towards Henry and smiled.

'Only the most stupid of the flock would go into the woods and I wouldn't bother to rescue it, even if I could hear it bleating. It wouldn't be much of a loss.'

At the end of lunch Henry pushed away his dish leaving the last corner of lemon meringue pie uneaten.

'Not hungry today?' His uncle's tone was accusatory.

'Yes. It's just . . .'

'Just what?' The old man scooped up the remains and popped them greedily into his mouth. He chewed with vigour. 'It seems all right to me.'

'Oh, it's all right.' Henry felt his heart miss a beat. He swallowed nervously. He wondered if his uncle could see the blood racing in a vein in his neck. He forced himself to meet his uncle's eyes and then noticed a minute smear of the violent yellow jelly left on the other's chin. 'I just don't like it,' he said.

For a moment his uncle stared at him, outraged, as though they had been arguing about something of earth-shattering importance. Then he turned abruptly and left the kitchen, muttering.

Henry ran all the way to the caravan park, eager to boast of his victory, but when Stella opened the door he realized that he would sound utterly ludicrous. She wouldn't care one bit about the battle of the lemon meringue.

'About that beach,' he panted instead, 'where you said there were currents. You said you'd show me. So I wondered . . .'

'Why not?' She looked really pleased and in a moment they were setting off, Mrs Elder calling after them to take care.

'Don't worry,' he called back. 'I'll look after her.'

'Look after me! That's rich. If anyone needs looking after, it's you, Henry Constable.'

'Rubbish,' he said cheerfully, knowing that she was right. The other night he had dreamt of resting his head in her lap and of her bending over him.

She went on ahead, through the meadows and up towards the cliffs, past the lions' enclosure and there, where the narrow cliff path turned left, she disappeared to the right.

'Stella?' He thought he had missed her: there seemed to be no path. He spun round, undecided. A smell of decay drifted over from the old lion who stood close to the fence – or was he resting against it? Below he heard water. He parted the undergrowth that grew very densely there and saw her half-way down the rocky side of the ravine. So this was where the River Rox finally ran into the sea. There were large boulders everywhere and the river, which was wider and sluggish further up, ran more swiftly here in the narrow channels, then suddenly disappeared underground. The noise he had heard came from where one of the many channels cut down deeply into the huge bank of black and grey pebbles.

'Wait! Stella, wait!'

She didn't, but moved on again, out of the shadows towards the brilliance of the sea which he could hear thundering beyond this great, grey bank. Over on the far side Henry saw the edge of the mesh fence shimmering in the sun. Then there was nothing at all.

He ran at the bank, making the pebbles shift and groan as he raced to get to the top first, but she beat him and let herself slide down the other side only coming to rest a few feet above a sweep of deep, swift-flowing water.

He had expected a beach but there wasn't one. There was just this, where the river water silently re-emerged and flowed unseen into the sea. He settled himself beside her, propped up against the shingle bank. The sun shone into his face and dazzled him and it was as wonderful as she had promised. For some minutes they were silent. Then she raised one arm against the sun and pointed with the other towards the white cliffs.

'That's where Julian painted them. See that overhang on the cliff? Well, at low tide you can go past it and round the headland and that's where he painted them.'

'Them?'

'A man and a woman.' She shivered in the sun.

'And you think it's that man's portrait, don't you?'

She nodded, moving her head up and down against the pebbles so that they rumbled gently.

'So he was here. With a woman.'

'Yes.'

'Where are they now? I mean, where's she?'

Stella shrugged.

Henry could barely breathe: the sun pressed down on him so fiercely that he shut his eyes and saw the ugly red stain of his own blindness. Then he remembered.

'That woman . . .'

'Yes?'

'In the picture you saw, did she have blue beads in her hair – sort of plaited in? Did she, Stella?'

'Yes – but how do *you* know that?'

'I think I've seen a picture of her. You see at home I've got this friend, Adam Draper – I think I've told you about him. He's the one with the mother. And this mother, Ali, sort of gave me one of Julian's portraits – because I'm a Constable. I mean, I know it sounds a bit complicated.'

'It certainly does.'

'But honestly, Stella, I think it could be a portrait of the same woman. In my picture, she's young and she's screaming with all this thick, black hair falling back and dragging her down, almost. And her hair is threaded with lines of little blue beads. It's turquoise blue, not that other blue, like in the flag. It could be her, couldn't it?'

Stella nodded and they looked along the indifferent white cliffs against which the high tide churned and broke.

'So,' Stella whispered, 'if she *was* here, what happened to her?'

Henry shook his head miserably: he did not want to think about it, especially not this afternoon which could be so perfect.

'You must ask your uncle, Henry.'

'I can't. I've tried, but he doesn't take any notice.'

'I bet you haven't said, "Who's that man in the woods?" '

'No.'

'Well you should. And then you should ask him what happened to the woman.'

'But I couldn't, Stella. He might think I thought –'

'And don't you?'

'No. No I don't. I mean, we don't even know that there ever was anybody else here. And that man – I mean – we don't *know* anything.'

'And you don't want to, do you?'

'I do.'

But she was right and they both knew it. She turned sharply from him. Her foot slipped on the shingle which shifted with an unhurried snarl, and she gasped as the pebbles that she snatched at came away and part of the great grey bank slithered down into the sea, taking her with it. Her feet were in the water and she was screaming now and he saw a stone strike her face. Her little ringed hands flailed as hopelessly as tarred wings and he shrank back in terror against the bank, and watched.

Chapter 14

She was sliding away from him.

'Stella, keep still!'

She didn't. Henry shouted again.

'Don't struggle – you'll go in deeper. Keep still!'

He didn't know if she had listened or even heard but fortunately she was still. The stones settled like some beast lying down, and she rested against them, panting. Her shoulders were still out of the water, but she was as still as someone who had drowned.

'Come on, Stella. Crawl. Crawl up, but slowly. Move slowly!' He feared that another sudden movement from either of them might cause the bank to collapse again. He made her go sideways to lessen the risk, and resisted the terrible temptation to lean down and help. Only when she was safely over the top did he follow, worming himself back up inch by inch.

'Thanks,' she whispered.

He shrugged.

'No, honestly.' She was flicking the grit and seaweed from her jeans, emptying out her shoes. 'I'd have gone right in. I'd have drowned, if it wasn't for you.'

'You wouldn't.'

'I would. Because of the currents. It's really dangerous here. Underneath, the river water is running out to sea, even on an incoming tide. I'd have drowned, honestly.'

'You wouldn't.' She'd only got wet, after all.

'I might. Or been buried.' She was shivering.

'Rubbish.'

Below her was the dark grey patch where the uncovered layer of shingle was still wet and cold. He imagined her little ringed hands sticking out and bruised.

'I don't know what to say, Henry.' She was uncharacteristically subdued.

He didn't want to be a hero and didn't feel like one, though it seemed to have ended all right. And if he had done the right thing it had only been luck. He still felt a failure: a miserable, cowardly failure. He had just stood there and watched, paralysed by the fear that if he moved to help her, his bit of the bank might have started to slide too. Some hero.

She was shivering violently and her lips were blue. He should have put his arms round her, offered his dry shirt, even chased her about so that she warmed up, but he didn't. She crouched there on the stones, her teeth chattering, and Henry, the hero, avoided her glance. He despised himself: a modern couch-potato hero who watched the world flash by and didn't, couldn't, do one single useful thing. And would lose his chance for ever –

'Stella, I've been thinking about that man in the wood and all that, and I know what to do now. And I'm sure I'm right, Stella, even if you don't agree with me. I'm absolutely sure, this time.'

She looked at him with tearful eyes and rubbed her hands over the darkened crest of hair so that drops of water flew off. There was disquiet in her eyes, but he ignored it.

'I'm going to set that man free. I've thought it all out. I'm going to get him out of here, make him leave, if I have to, take him to the police or the authorities, or people like that.

134

Then he can talk to them, tell them what happened. And if there was another person with him, he can explain. I mean, it's up to him, isn't it? And don't you say that maybe he can't speak the language, because the authorities always have interpreters. And places for people like him to go – '

'Great!' She got up, wiped off the tears, and wrung out her socks. 'Great!'

She really was impossible.

'You don't understand,' he cried.

'I do. It'd be from one prison to another.'

'Rubbish. You're *so* stupid, Stella. So stupid!' How could anyone he loved be so hateful? How could she mock him like that?

'You mustn't do this,' she pleaded, still shivering, cradling herself in her arms. 'We don't know what's happened in the past. Ask your uncle first. Give him a chance.'

'I thought you hated my uncle, like you hate *all* the Constables. Oh yes, I remember. You said that we spoilt things. Well, you're wrong and I'm going to show you. I'm going to put things right. I'm not going to stand back and let things happen and pretend that I never knew. Unlike some people in Roxmere Park.'

She looked down, as though ashamed, as though *she* had mistaken the figure on a stormy night.

'I'm going to do something about this,' he yelled and he heard his voice echoing against the cliffs.

'Yes, but not like that. Please, Henry. Talk to your uncle.'

'Oh, shut up, for heaven's sake.' Maybe she wasn't so pretty, after all: her teeth weren't very straight.

'Anyway,' he said, 'why don't you ask him yourself, or are you afraid to lose that precious job of your mother's? Go on, you ask. I dare you.'

'All right.'

'But you can't. You mustn't. I mean, or you could lose that job . . .'

'I'll have to risk that, won't I?'

She put on her socks and shoes, fumbling with the wet, knotted laces.

'Stella!'

But she stumbled off, scattering the shingle, leaving the ruined afternoon behind her. If only she'd look back. Then he could have caught up with her and explained, raced her up the ravine, beaten her easily and helped her up that last steep bit, because she must be feeling shaky after what nearly happened.

Oh Stella, Stella. But she didn't look back. So he'd have to show her, show all of them, show the whole world.

He turned away to wipe the sea spray off his face and saw something further along the shore. A greyish bundle, like rags only heavier, had floated in on the tide. It turned slowly round and round and when the waves withdrew would be left there, with the bits of wood and plastic bottles and frayed coils of orange nylon rope. He guessed, from the way it turned and spun, that there was more below the water and he thought he smelt it, but didn't go and look – hadn't got the time, as he would be busy with the man in the wood. Later he'd tell his uncle casually, 'Actually, Uncle Arthur, I know what happened to the goats, or one of them anyway: it drowned off the shingle bank.' He'd face his uncle squarely, man to man. He'd make his uncle look away. His old face would be haunted by guilt if he had any memory of a young woman with blue beads in her hair who had also drowned there. Now, though, he had to find the man.

He followed the river as far into the woods as he could. In parts the water was very low. Anybody could easily have waded across and scrambled up the bank to the mesh fence, but he didn't bother. As he went in more deeply he started to move more cautiously, watching for signs, listening for sounds of the mallet or the axe. Several times he was sure that he'd walked in a circle.

He wished he'd brought money, for a bus or taxi, but it was too late now. He'd flag down the first car that came along. Anybody would stop, seeing him with such a man. It was still hot even in the shade of the trees. He would have liked a drink, but didn't dare kneel down to scoop up some water. Somebody spoke. Henry hesitated, unable to hear clearly because of the pounding in his ears as he leant over the river. There wasn't anyone there. Behind him the floor of leaves was untouched. No twig moved and the gnats swung up and down under the outstretched branches as though someone had reached in and twisted round the thick, warmed air. Maybe no one had spoken. He crawled under hazel that had fallen to one side, like an arch.

Then he saw the man. He was leaning casually against a trunk, his arms folded, his feet sunk into the leaves, as though he had been there some time, as though he might have been waiting for someone to come by. Henry was encouraged.

'You have to come with me, now. Out of here.' Henry pointed to some invisible distance beyond the fence. He said it again, speaking louder and more slowly, feeling a little foolish, since the man probably didn't understand, but he wasn't going to be defeated. He beckoned with his finger, smiling encouragingly, as you do with children.

'Come along,' he said, 'please.'

He hadn't contemplated failure, had only thought of being beyond the wall and out on the bright, sunlit road to freedom. He would have taken the other's hand, would have led him away, had the man not continued to lean against the tree with his arms still folded. There were leaves caught in his hair, and patches where mud or sweat had soaked into his shirt and dried. Poor fool.

It was all so wrong, so desperately, miserably wrong.

'Please,' he begged. 'You *must* come.'

'Why?'

'Because my uncle says so. My uncle, Arthur Constable. He sent me. He says that you must come with me. Now.'

'I'll come.' The man spoke slowly, unwillingly.

It wasn't, Henry told himself, really a lie. It was something he had to do, for the man's sake. He'd explain later, apologize if necessary. It wasn't as though he was being dishonest: he was helping someone who couldn't help himself.

'You *do* understand?' He hadn't appreciated what had happened for a moment. 'You *spoke*? So you *do* understand?'

'Of course.'

'So, why . . . why?'

Now, suddenly, it was impossible to ask the questions. Instead he made his way frantically towards the hidden gate in the wall. The man followed, but reluctantly, as though he was doing a favour.

'Hurry. I mean, please could you go a bit quicker? My uncle's waiting.'

The man did not alter his pace. Henry looked back, constantly afraid that the other would just disappear, just turn away and vanish. He wasn't going to give up this time. Any moment now they'd be through the gate. Beyond the wall, it would be all right. He turned the key in the lock. Stella would be so surprised: she probably thought he'd funk it at the last minute. But he hadn't. She'd never call him a creep again.

The first car didn't stop, didn't even brake, though he waved wildly. Henry shrugged apologetically at the man, who had wandered after him. He had ambled through the gate and now frowned at the hot road and the roar of a lorry labouring up the hill. This time Henry ran into the road, but the driver only shook his head and went on. The man turned back and stood in the shade of the wall. He leant against it, bored.

'It won't be a minute, honestly.' Henry was disappointed that the other was so unenthusiastic. Then the next car slowed, and the driver smiled as he wound down the window. Suddenly he looked from Henry to the man, wound up the window and accelerated away.

'I'm awfully sorry, I expect they're busy,' apologized Henry. He remembered unhappily that his parents never stopped for hitch-hikers. Maybe if the man went back through the gate – just for a moment, because he did look very scruffy, to be honest. Anybody like his parents would be bound to think he was a tramp or a wino, and would not want to take him.

'I'm sure somebody will stop in a moment.'

The man folded his arms and almost smiled. He said something in that other language, then: 'You lie.'

'No! No, honestly. It isn't like you think – I mean, my uncle didn't actually say . . .'

Another car flashed by, then another old lorry crawled to the top of the hill, lumbering and swaying, followed by a trail of impatient, irritated vehicles. Their exhaust fumes stank. Henry stepped back: it was as foul and relentless as the rush-hour at home.

'I'll get help – from the next lot.'

'Help?'

'Yes – for you. Help for you – to get away from here.'

The man unfolded his arms and looked at his hands. He touched the cracked calluses in the palms with his finger-tips and shook his head. Maybe they were painful. Poor thing. No wonder people like Mrs Ferris had thought there was a devil in the woods. Maybe this man did look threatening.

'We could start walking . . . to Roxmere . . . if you like? I'll show you what to do.'

The man smiled, then laughed, and turned away. He went back through the gate and called in a low voice, 'No. You come, Henry Constable, you come with me and I will show you!'

With all the glory of his expected triumph utterly gone, Henry could only follow. The man moved with the careful skill of one who knows every metre of the land. He pressed on without looking back, and soon Henry was sure that they were returning to the sea. Now and then Henry hung behind uncertainly. He feared that this was unwise and unsuitable. He'd heard all the scare stories a thousand times and this man was a real stranger, and was strong. Henry's legs ached: he'd been dashing around for most of the afternoon. Whatever happened, he wasn't going along the cliff path with this man. He'd just run off.

The man followed a path similar to Stella's, but instead of making for the shingle bank he kept close to the base of the white cliffs so that the exposed headland stretched in front of them. The tide had turned. The thousands and millions of mussels which clung to the rocks were now free from the pounding foam and they were as blue and bright as snatches of summer sky behind torn storm clouds. With the outgoing tide, a way round the headland was revealed. The man climbed over into the next bay.

Henry nearly didn't follow, nearly turned back and ran, but in the end kept on and only wished, passionately, that

Stella had been there. She would have given him courage.

They climbed over the last boulder and jumped down on to a tiny, wet beach which the sea had just left. Then he saw the statues. There were hundreds of them, maybe more than hundreds. Every surface of smooth rock and every boulder above sea level had either an image etched into it or a sculpture set upon it. It was a gallery grown from the sea.

Henry couldn't speak. There were more carvings set on niches carved out of the chalk cliffs. Some clearly had not been safe enough, for though the headland protected this small cove, storms or neap tides had dashed down many of the figures and they lay there between the other flotsam of the shore: a worn down face, a limb half buried beneath shining, leathery fronds of seaweed, a bit of shoe, green rope and the heavy timbers of sunken ships.

'Will I leave this?' the man asked, and said more, too, that Henry could not understand.

He shook his head instead of replying. It was like nothing he had ever imagined: a world recreated and a universe fashioned and cast down. Some pieces were beautiful, so, so beautiful. Some were not. Some clearly told a story, but he did not know if it was of tragedy or joy. There were carvings in stone and chalk and wood. He reached out and touched the figure of a young woman, ran his fingers up her spine and closed his hand over her head, which was cold and wet. He pushed aside a trail of bright green weed. An hour ago it had been submerged and would be again, would be in the end quite worn down.

Then he remembered. He had visited this world before. On another still afternoon when he had only been a very little boy he had run his hand over the surface, but been frightened. This time he was not. Having come so far, he would not now turn back.

'She was . . . your wife?'

The other nodded.

'And she died? Here?'

'Yes. There.' He pointed. For one dreadful moment Henry thought that he would see her, caught between rocks, with her long hair still braided with blue beads.

He was pointing to a rock that the sea had barely left. He must have worked his story into it years ago, because already some parts had been covered by barnacles. Others had been ground away by the tides, but the record was still there. A couple were leaving a faraway land, a wooded land, and they travelled by boat, with her hair blowing in the wind and his eyes looking up at the stars above. Then surely, these were the hazel woods, as light and delicate as ferns. There was the house and then, surely, that was the drowning, at the base of the cliffs, in sight but beyond the help of another man who stood on the shore and watched; who stretched out his hands, but who could not find hers amidst the turmoil of the waves.

Sea water still trickled down over this face of rock that was marked with the bright stains of iron and the steely glitter of quartz. Henry squatted down, trying to see more clearly. He felt along the lines with the tips of his fingers. He felt the face.

'It's my uncle,' he whispered, guessing more than knowing.

'Yes.'

'And you?'

'I was not there.'

'Why?'

The man shrugged and turned away.

'But I am here now,' he said, 'always.'

'I . . . I think I should go. Please. If that's all right. Before the tide comes in. If you don't mind.'

'You go.'
'And you?'
'I? Oh, I stay.'
'Yes. Yes, I see. And I'm sorry. Really, truly sorry.'

Chapter 15

He burst into the hall, determined to ask.

Arthur Constable was already there. Henry clung to the front door, panting. The old man stood in front of the photo, gazing at his younger self. Then, disregarding Henry, he stepped closer and stretched out an old, trembling hand, as though he would have parted the branches and pushed back the lush black leaves and finally seen through more clearly.

'Uncle Arthur.'

'I never – ' retorted his uncle, starting and staggering a little. The face he let his great-nephew glimpse was frail, irresolute and full of sadness. The soft skin around his mouth that was habitually drawn up into that taut, keen smile had slackened. A thread of spit hung from his old, pale lips.

'Uncle Arthur, are you all right?' Henry was disconcerted: something seemed to have happened to the old boy.

Arthur Constable recovered himself. He ran his hand smartly over his face and curved up the corners of his mouth. Then he turned his back on the picture, straightened up and stood with his feet apart and his hands on his hips as if ready to take on all comers.

'Ah, Henry!' His voice was so bright, one could imagine it snapping off.

There was a noise in the kitchen and for a moment Henry thought he smelt buttered toast. He imagined biting into a crisp corner.

'Just the man I was looking for. Henry, how about phoning them at home, eh? I think it would be an excellent idea, don't you? And you might as well do it now. No time like the present, eh? There you are, all you've got to do is dial.' He smiled encouragingly.

The unexpected suggestion caught Henry off guard, threw him from the scent, as it were, and as if in a dream he obeyed his uncle. He picked up the receiver and dialled as he had been told, but did it wrong. His hands shook, he tried again and then again and got through, it seemed, but no one answered. Surely somebody would be at home, even if it was only Ed. He wouldn't have minded that, not now.

'Hello . . .' he began. Something wasn't right.

'Hello?' It wasn't his house or his family. As in a nightmare he recognized the voice but could not remember properly.

'Hello? Tom? Ed?' After all, phones do distort voices, like tape recorders. He'd even been mistaken for his mother a couple of times.

'Hello?' Had they gone? Had they taken the opportunity of his absence to vanish for ever? Had they moved house in the night to free themselves from the irritation he caused under their nails? The pain was sudden, like twisting your ankle. Through the agony he heard Adam Draper laugh with surprise.

'Why, you rotten dog,' drawled Adam. 'Thanks for remembering me. At last!'

'I've been busy.'

'Come on, Henry! You busy? Don't give me that. It's *me*, Adam, you're talking to.'

'Honestly, Adam, all sorts of things have been going on down here.'

'Such as?'

'Well . . .' He was aware of his uncle watching and listening.

'I . . . I've been helping my uncle with his reports and . . . and . . . I met this girl, Stella.'

'Now he tells me! You dirty dog. So it's like that, is it? And up here your poor mother has been going round the bend with worry about her darling Henry. Whenever she phones your uncle says that you're either asleep or out in the park and that he can't get you.'

'You mean my mother's phoned a lot?'

'Obviously.'

He heard his uncle clear his throat.

'She's even been round here, asking if I'd had news from you,' laughed Adam.

'Really?' That was surprising. Jean Constable would chat to Ali Draper if they met in the street, and she nodded and smiled over the front garden that had gone to ruin and let down the street, everybody said. She never 'went round' to the Drapers.

'Well come on, Henry, what have you really been up to, down there?'

'Nothing much.' He glanced across at his uncle, who had taken off his glasses and was polishing them slowly. The old man caught his eye, beamed, popped his glasses back on and came close, as though he had just been struck by an extraordinary idea.

'I say, Henry, how about fixing the exact date for your return? I expect you're missing them, eh? I'll tell you what, Henry,' he said, putting an arm around him, 'you could go tomorrow. I'll run you down to the station myself. How about it?' He was almost begging.

Henry moved away.

'Henry? You still there?' asked Adam.

His uncle was trying to get rid of him.

'Henry?' Ali Draper's music drifted down the phone line.

'Why didn't you tell me that my mother had phoned?'

'I did . . .' His uncle was taken aback.

'Only that first time.'

'I didn't want you to be homesick, Henry. After all, I went to boarding school when I was six, I know all about being homesick. If you let children talk to their parents all the time, it upsets them. Makes them cry.'

'I'm not six, and you should have told me.'

'Rubbish. But I did it for the best. I wanted you to be happy here.'

'And now you want to get rid of me.'

'Of course I don't. I wanted you to understand what I was doing here. I wanted to give you a chance, let you get away from home, escape the family, your mother, escape being blamed. I thought that was what you wanted. I thought you were bored at home.'

In a way it was true. It would have been easier to pretend that everything his uncle said was a lie, but it wasn't so. It had been wonderful to get away. It had felt like escape. Not always, of course, but often.

'But you should have told me, Uncle Arthur.'

'Told you! Told you what? There's nothing to tell.' His anger was frightening. Distantly Henry heard Adam asking again if everything was all right, and from the kitchen, someone unmistakably moved crockery around, put cups on saucers maybe, and poured water. Something had definitely happened.

In the cool stone hall Henry replaced the receiver. He would phone home later. Now he went over to the photo and touched the shadowing leaves, as if to pull them apart.

'You should have told me about this man.'

'How dare you . . .' snarled Arthur Constable.

But Henry wasn't going to be frightened off. He had hold of the branches now and was not going to let them spring back. Outside, the tide would soon turn and the waters would be slowly rising, hiding it all again.

'You should have told me about this man, Uncle, this man in the woods.'

'Get out. Get out now, you ungrateful little fool.'

'No, Uncle Arthur. Tell me.'

'She's put you up to this, hasn't she? That wretched woman and her daughter. Is this all the thanks I get for giving her a home and a job? She's spread malicious gossip about me. Do you think I don't know what they say in the village? Well, it's all lies, Henry. Ugly lies.'

The old man fumbled at the collar of his shirt. Beads of sweat had sprung out on his forehead and the lines of his face crumbled like ashes. He looked as though he were going to fall down. Staggering to the foot of the stairs, he clung there like one who has been struck hard but will stay on his feet whatever the cost. Somewhere in the house a door swung and banged as a gust of wind stirred the smell of dust.

Had Stella already said something and was that why his uncle wanted to pack him off home?

'Uncle?' He approached the uncertain figure as warily as one does an injured animal. Suddenly, painfully, he felt pity. It seemed that the old man's defiance had gone.

'Uncle? Can I get someone? Julian, or Mrs Elder?'

'No.' Arthur Constable shook his head and Henry felt his own anger fade away.

'Come on, Uncle Arthur. You can tell me.' It was like speaking to a child.

'No! You wouldn't understand. Nobody understands!' His voice was querulous and petulant. He even sniffed.

'Try and tell me. Honestly, Uncle, I *do* want to know. I really *am* interested.'

It was true and he heard himself with surprise, as though he were listening to someone else.

'I've never been really interested in anything before. At home, like I said, everything was so boring and I never wanted to do anything – well, not what everybody else wanted to do anyway – but it's different here. I'm not bored here! And I am interested, honestly.'

It was as though something had fallen away from him. Something that had bound him and held him down had split or cracked or been thrown off, like an outgrown skin. It was like growing taller overnight: the sort of thing one dreamed of when one was nine. He took the old man's hand, and patted it awkwardly where the bulging blue veins crawled over the thin flesh. Poor old fool.

'I never meant it to happen,' whined Uncle Arthur. 'And I still maintain that I was right. Essentially right, even if there were problems along the way. After all, everybody has problems, don't they, Henry? And problems are there to be overcome.' His voice had strengthened as he spoke; his courage was returning, his ability to deceive himself revived. Some colour returned to his face.

'Now look here, Henry, you don't really want to hear about an old man's problems, do you?' He was already seeking out an escape route, like a rat in a rising flood.

'Yes I do. And you're going to tell me about the man in the wood. I've spoken to him, Uncle. I've seen the statues.'

Arthur Constable slumped back. Wearily he waved his arm at the photos around the walls.

'These were all taken in the first year here, the year the park opened. It was that glorious summer. I was one of the very first, Henry, if not the first, to try and keep wild animals in a natural habitat. You see how my lions roamed freely then? But it wasn't just that. My vision was wider – still is, Henry. Nobody has proved me wrong, yet – and when my book is published, when I really explain my theories, everybody will see I'm right.'

'About the man, Uncle? And the woman?'

'I was explaining, if you hadn't interrupted. They were part of my vision, Henry. Oh yes. They *wanted* to come. I didn't force them. Nobody can accuse me of that. Oh no. They *asked* to come. Of course I'd known him for years, since he was a little lad. He'd been at one of the mission schools near where I was doing my research; he was such a bright lad – good with his hands too, always there to help around the camp. I could see that he was special, but I could also see that in a few years he'd be spoiled.'

'What do you mean, spoiled?'

'Spoiled by us, Henry, spoiled by our way of life. And that's when I decided to bring him back with me. All people, Henry, have their place in the world. And should stay there. I was offering this young man and his wife the chance to survive – to stay in their place. I was offering them – everything.'

'What? How could you be offering them "everything" when you were shutting them up in your park, like animals in a zoo!'

'You haven't understood. We all have our place: plants, fish, men, women – and humans need to be protected as much as other species. I was giving them the chance to live a perfect life, a traditional life, to remain true to themselves, to resist change. I admired them, Henry. I wanted other people to admire them as they were.' He sighed irritably and Henry stared at him in horrified silence.

'What happened?' he whispered finally.

'Nothing happened.'

'That's not true. She drowned, didn't she?'

'No. It was an accident. She didn't know about the dangerous currents around the cliffs. She shouldn't have tried to swim there anyway. I had warned her. But she would go there, day after day; she used to sit out on those rocks and gaze out to sea and wait. It wasn't my fault, Henry, if she waited for the tide to sweep in. Nobody can blame me. I tried my best to save her, but she was carried away beyond my grasp. And after that, he changed. He gave up. The more I urged him to forget, to concentrate on recreating his traditions here, the more he withdrew from my plans and made his own. Now he won't leave these woods, he's made a shrine to her, he won't forget. And it's made such trouble for me, Henry. People talk. There's all sorts of ugly gossip in the village. I even had to close the park. And that ignorant man, Henry, that man who knew nothing, has adapted his whole way of life, and lives in my woods as though he owns them. It's intolerable. I've been betrayed. He could have proved all my theories, but he wouldn't, Henry, he just wouldn't.'

'Maybe your theories aren't right.'

'That's impossible. Quite impossible. I *know* I'm right.'

'But . . .' He fought for words, but found none that could say what was in his heart.

'I can see that you don't understand,' the old man sniffed. 'I hoped you would, but I was wrong in that too. You're just like all the rest. Even my son doesn't understand. He takes my money and hates me. He won't even paint what I want him to, though I'm paying for the wretched paint. But I'll prove I'm right. Just you wait and see.'

He pushed his spectacles back up his nose, pulled himself up and hurried off into his study as though he were about to sit down and begin the impossible task that very moment.

Henry stayed on in the hall, his heart pounding and pounding. It was all so awful. So utterly futile. So wrong – and he was so powerless.

'Stella?'

She was waiting for him in the kitchen, a tray of tea things in her hands. She must have heard. She must know that he'd totally failed – once again.

'I made it for him,' she said oddly, looking down at the toast and biscuits.

'Why?'

'I felt sorry for him. I had a go at him, about that man. And he told me to shut up and I told him that he was a heartless, unfeeling egoist – it was an awful row, and he looked so feeble and ill, that I thought I'd sort of say – well, sorry.'

'You? Say sorry?'

'Yes. Funny isn't it? But I am, Henry. I am sorry for him. I mean, you were wonderful in there, talking to him – you didn't lose your temper, or yell daft things like me. You're just the sort of person he should listen to – but of course, he won't. He can't. And that's sad. Really sad.' She had tears in her eyes, real brimming tears that suddenly ran over and down her cheeks in black trails of mascara which she licked at, the tray still clutched in her little ringed hands.

'Stella?'

'It isn't anything. It's this beastly old dusty house. It gets in my eyes.'

He would have thrown his arms around her if it wasn't for the tray. She wiped her mouth and nose on her sleeve and he loved her with an intensity that he had never even imagined.

Later, he would phone home properly and see how everyone was up there. He could tell his mother, with complete honesty, that he was missing her cooking. He could tell them that he was missing Ed's jokes and that, now that he thought about it, when Tom went up to university he would, after all, like to move into his room. There would be space there to put up the portrait. And Ed could have his old room, with the hiding place which he was pretty sure his younger brother had discovered anyway. And tomorrow he and Stella could maybe go down into the village and see Mrs Ferris again. They could even arrange to travel back to Clapham Junction together. First, though, they had to take the tea in to Uncle Arthur, before the toast went as hard as rock.

He took the tray from her and went into his uncle's study for the first time, expecting to find the old man immersed in his research. Instead, a large desk strewn with abandoned, dust-covered papers stood neglected in one dark corner. Arthur Constable stood by the window. His forehead and the palms of his hands were pressed against the glass and he stared out over the wonderful, beautiful park with the dull eyes of one who has been captive too long.

Henry set down the tray and silently crept out. In the kitchen Stella had rubbed away her tears.

'Tomorrow,' he said, 'at low tide, we can go round the headland into the bay.'

'All right,' she said. 'But I'm warning you. If it's sunny, I'll wear that dress.'

153

Also by Gaye Hiçyılmaz

The Frozen Waterfall

Winner of the Writers' Guild Award Best Children's
Book 1994

Shortlisted for the Smarties Award and Guardian
Young Fiction Award 1994

'Surely the outstanding novel of the season. Selda (12)
leaves Turkey with her mother and sisters to join her
(dominating) father in Switzerland. She is an independent
who wants to learn all she can in school and out, and this,
against all odds, she does. She acquires unlikely friends: a
rich, elegant classmate, unhappy at home, and an illegal
immigrant young boy; they become a trio. But the larger
world invades even family life. A find for readers who
welcome long books with living themes.' Naomi Lewis,
Observer

'. . . an outstanding novel, as quietly compelling as The
Diary of Anne Frank . . .' *The Tablet*